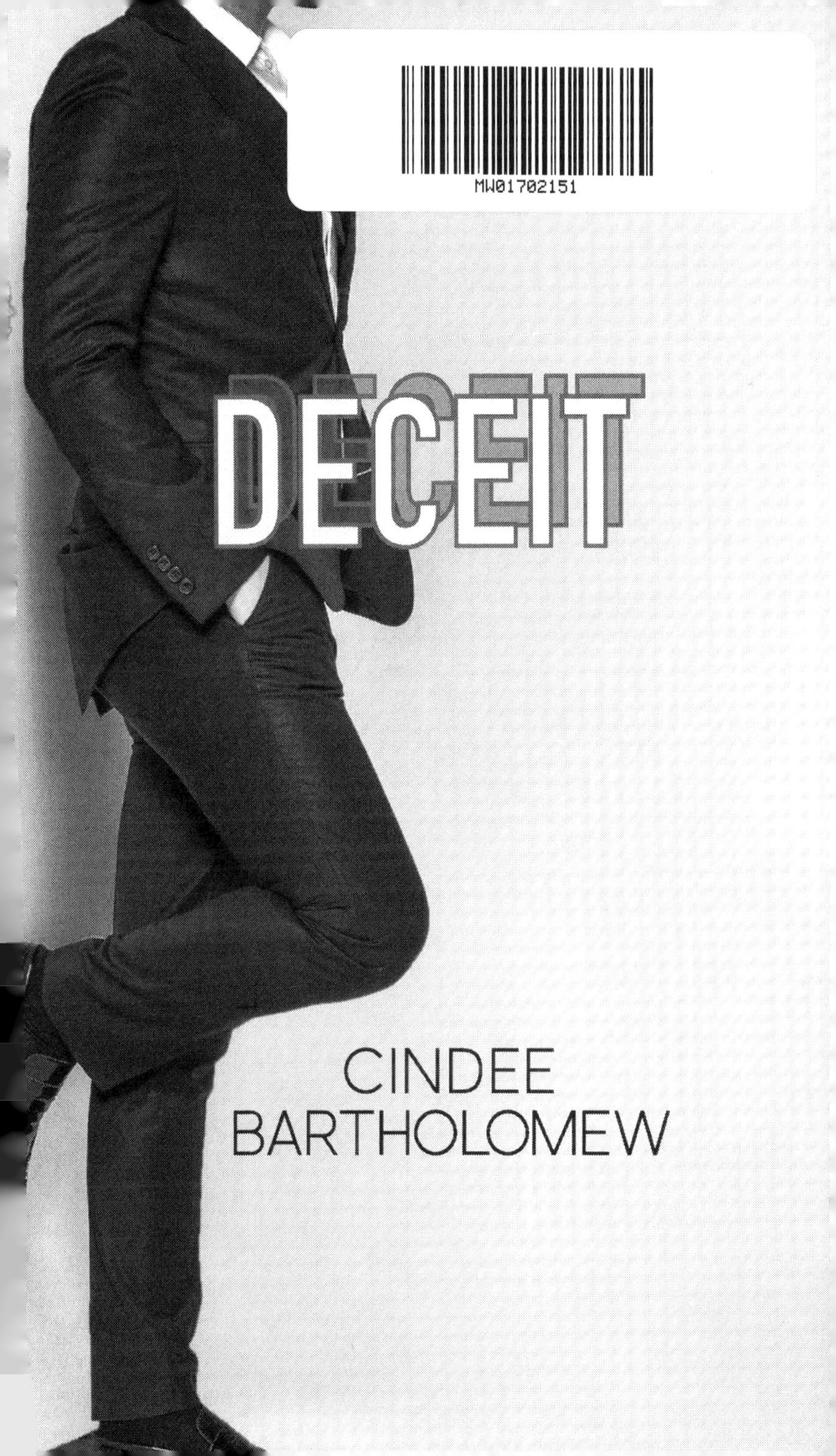
MW01702151
DECEIT
CINDEE
BARTHOLOMEW

AUTHOR'S COPYRIGHT

This is a work of fiction. Names, characters, organizations, places, events, and incidents are either products of the author's imagination or are used fictitiously. Any resemblance to actual events, locales, or persons living or dead are entirely coincidental.

Copyright © 2023 Cindee Bartholomew ALL RIGHTS RESERVED

No part of this book may be reproduced, or stored in a retrieval system, or transmitted in any form or by any means electronic, mechanical, photocopying, recording, or otherwise, without express written permission of the publisher.

This book is licensed for your personal enjoyment only. This book may not be re-sold or given away to other people.

Formatting by: Jessika Klide, LLC

Published in the United States of America

CONTENTS

A NOTE TO THE READER

Cindee first penned this romance in 2014 under her pen name, Jessika Klide.

This edition is no less steamy with its sensual prose, but this version is without the 'hardcore' plot.

To Curtis, my soulmate, my Golden God.

Without his forever love, this story could not have been written.

He is my 'every thang.' ;)

CHAPTER ONE

Rome, Italy

Maximus Aurelius Moore

THE MUTED SOUNDS of the early morning horns seep through the walls as traffic begins to congest on the city street below. Today is the third day of my fourteen-day leave.

It's been a challenge maintaining a dual lifestyle,

but I've successfully kept my Italian and American life separate. Here, I'm the most eligible bachelor in Italy, the heir to the Liotine Dynasty. In Alabama, my homeboys know I have money, but not the extent of it. To them, I'm just another American flyboy, Warrant Officer Aurelius Moore, AH-64 Apache pilot. And the satisfied woman sleeping beside me knows nothing about me.

Her deep, even breathing, with softly exhaled breaths, confirms she is in a peaceful, satisfied sleep. Glancing at her blissful expression, I gently pull my arm out from under the pillow, trying not to disturb her. She doesn't twitch, and that fact makes me chuckle softly. She called my name last night and didn't even know it.

Our session began from behind, impersonal. Slow and steady, letting her get used to my size as I reached around and played with her breasts. When I turned up my intensity, I had both hands and all my fingers working her erogenous zones, lightly tickling them.

Typically, this technique and my sheer volume give an immediate orgasm, but this girl didn't give me any signs of a growing need to explode. Having had sex with many women, I know not all can have orgasms. Some have physical issues that prevent it, poor souls. It was a tad disappointing because she had been fun up until then, and a nice distraction. But being one of those unfortunate women, there was no point in trying to please her. No man can thrust life into a lost cause, so I set about satisfying my needs.

When she screamed, it broke my pounding trance, and I was concerned my hammering had been too hard. I froze over her writhing body.

She lifted her face off the bed, cut her eyes back at me, and then sucked air in. "Per favore," her voice was desperate.

"It's ok. It's ok."

"Uff!" She dropped her head and panted loud. Her breath was labored.

I scanned her body, but there were no apparent signs that she was injured; however, there wouldn't be, so I asked her. "Are you okay?"

"Uff!" She shook her head violently from side to side, then beat the bed with her fist.

I leaned over to comfort her, but my gentle touch made her scream again. "Per favore," she cried.

"Tell me what is wrong!" I commanded her.

"Continuare. Per favore. Più forte! Più forte!" She buried her face in the covers, letting loose a barrage of muffled curse words.

I chuckled, relieved, then smacked her ass once hard to break her tantrum. "I misunderstood. I'm going to give you the fucking of a lifetime. But you need to calm down."

She froze, lifted her head, then turned to stare at me.

I smiled. "Let me know when you're ready to continue."

"Continue?" She pushed up on her elbows, and her eyes hunted my manhood. "Nessuna eiaculazione precoce?"

I laughed as I stoked my flagpole for her, "Sì, no premature ejaculation. I can go all night."

A grin broke out on her face. She rolled her eyes, collapsed on the bed, lifted her ass for me, spread her cheeks for access, and said, "Sono pronto per il cazzo di una vita."

I lined up to give her what she asked for, the fucking of a lifetime. "Ready?" I confirmed.

"Sì! Sì! Duro!"

Most women say they want it hard, but they really mean a firm thrust that bottoms out and lifts them off their toes. They want that deep spot they don't know they have massaged. Or they mean fast and furious. They do not mean as hard as I can pound. If I did that, I would crush them. I pride myself on my skill and technique. I like to watch them lose their shit repeatedly before I lose mine, and I do it repeatedly all night until they pass out from the pleasure I have given them.

I may not experience the deep love that other men do that makes them commit to a single woman, but I do love women. And I love satisfying them. That's my passion. Pleasing Princesses.

With one hand fisting her long hair and the other on her shoulder, I thrust deep, hard, and lifted her ass off the bed. Then I pumped and pounded her fast. The smacking sound of her ass being hammered hard and her moans as she got closer and closer fueled my fervor, and I pushed her over the top like the expert I am.

She fell forward, trying to collapse, but I didn't let her. Oh no. That girl almost lost her mind earlier from her fuckstration and cried for more. By God, that was exactly what I gave her. More of Moore! I pulled her body off the bed and sat her on my throbbing rod, then thrust her up in the air, making her bounce on my dick. The slamming sensation made her climax again.

When she finished, she fell forward. But I hadn't cum yet. So I draped her again over the footboard and eased in slow. I thrust into her at my own pace, and right before I blew my wad, she was whimpering like a porn star with another mind-blowing orgasm. Round one was done, then we moved to round two.

My phone vibrates.

I open my eyes and stare blankly at the ceiling.

I know it's important. Only a handful of people have this number, but, "Dammit," I could use another couple of hours of sleep. I rub my face, intentionally taking a few more seconds to clear the cobwebs before I check to see how my day will start.

Leaning on my elbow, I reach for it and peek at the screen to see who the text is from. It's Darren Martin, a longtime friend and venture capital partner. Sliding the screen open, I read the entire text.

> Call me when you have ten minutes to talk. I need a favor.

Collapsing into the pillows, I pull one under my head, then enjoy the view of the beauty's chest rise and fall. She's serene, lying here, her dark hair tousled, spilling over the white pillowcase. I trace my finger down her back, then give her ass a little squeeze. She was a good time and had a lot of stamina. She challenged me. I liked being pushed to perform.

She rolls away, not interested in anything but sleep, and snuggles with her pillow. I grin and roll onto my back to stretch. My hand touches the top of the headboard, and I search for the camera strap. Rolling over, I drag my body over the sheets to peer down between the headboard and the mattress. It's wedged between them.

How the hell did it end up there? No telling. She lost her frustration in round one, her inhibitions in round two, and in round three, we explored different positions.

Pulling the camera out, I sit up and bring it to my eye to focus, then turn it on my subject, and snap the last couple of photographs of her shoot. Capturing her peacefulness.

Knowing it won't last, I sigh and lower the camera to my lap. Flipping through the pics, I scan the photos. I got some excellent action shots and perfect "O" faces.

I smirk. I wish I could have captured her 'Oh my god, you want me to suck that big dick?' face. That would have been priceless.

I chuckle. She turned out to be an exceptionally fun one. I'll need to tell Adona how much I enjoyed her.

The need to piss asserts itself, so I set the camera

on the nightstand next to my phone, toss the covers over her nakedness, and bend down to pick up the used condoms from the floor. Her phone is lying next to them. I throw it on the nightstand, too, then go to the bathroom to relieve my bladder and brush my teeth. When I come back out, I go to the bar, grab a water, then pull up a chair to hydrate while I wait for her to wake, dreading the next part.

She was fun, and as much as I would love to say the words, "Let's do it again." I can't. That would be a lie, and I'm not a liar. I sit in silence, watching her breathe, knowing the sad reality of my truth is that I don't do repeats. I twist the top off the bottle of water and take a swig. It would be so nice if I could say, 'You were great, and I enjoyed myself. Thanks. Ciao.' Kiss each other's cheeks, and leave with smiles plastered across our faces, but that never happens.

I put the top back on and stare at her without seeing her. They always want to see me again. What can I say? I smirk. I'm that good. I'm the whole package. I not only seduce their bodies, but I seduce their minds too. Seduction is a true art form. Augustus taught me that.

I twist the top off, take several long swallows, then put it back on.

Being models, not prostitutes, I've had to hone

my skill, not having the luxury of time for courtship. I smirk again. I begin their seduction the moment they enter the studio. I learned quickly that it isn't always what you say but the subtlety of what you do that makes a woman feel special and works magic on her—getting inside her head, penetrating her mind first, caressing her there, letting her feel you deep inside her subconscious mind, seducing her, then calling out to her wild side. All the while, your body language is dominating her from a safe distance, demanding her attention but not overwhelming her with your masculinity. Slowly giving her a little taste of your power to control her but not commanding her yet.

Ummm. I love that. Nothing is more satisfying than watching them melt before you. When you start touching and tasting them, their wildness purrs, and that's when you start taming them.

That's a powerful drug! The look in their eyes when they have reached their limit, the way their bodies wither under you, needing what only you can give them. A screaming orgasm. Ummm. Ain't nothing better than that.

I twist the top off the water bottle, drink half, and put it back on.

Damn! I sound like a cocky son of a bitch. But

the brutal, hardcore truth is —I am that good. That's the real reason why they get all bent out of shape when they expect to see me again, and I tell them no.

I stare at the raven-haired beauty in the bed, then drain the water bottle and resist the temptation to squeeze it, knowing the noise will wake her. I twirl the empty bottle around in my fingers instead.

Even though I'm alright with my setup, it doesn't mean I'm not lonely and wouldn't enjoy a steady relationship. But I'm different; my desires are different. Finding someone like me is so far off the charts of possible even a Vegas gambler wouldn't take the odds. I've never felt that undeniable spark that drives a man to hook up with one woman in a steady, long-term relationship.

I thought I did the first summer I hooked up with a girl whose name I can't remember now. I banged and banged and banged her, then banged her some more. I grin. I thought I was in love, but I wasn't even in lust. I was a horny teenage boy with an amped-up sex drive who loved doing the deed. When she returned to college, I returned to middle school and moved on.

At first, I tried the whole dating scene, which was a fiasco. The drama was off the charts, with no banging to ease the pain.

I chuckle, remembering a conversation I had with my sister, Ann.

"Ann, what's wrong with answering, 'Hell yeah!' when she asks me, 'Does my ass look big in these pants?' That's a compliment. Not an insult."

Ann laughed, and I got pissed off. "What? It was. She has a big ass, and it's great!"

"Aurelius, girls want it curved."

"That's right! I want her ass curved too!"

"No, no."

"Yes, yes!"

"No, brother. They want the truth curved, not straight line like that."

"What the hell are you talking about?"

"Girls want you to tell them. 'Your ass is perfect.'"

"I did!"

"No. You told her that her ass was huge!" She rolled off the bed laughing at me.

"It is!" I laughed too.

"Girls want you to lie to them with the same lies they tell themselves."

"Well, I ain't no damn liar."

"Well, you don't have to lie, really. Just learn her love language."

My 'what the hell does that mean' look made her die laughing again.

"Never tell another woman as long as you live that their ass is big, and you'll be ok."

"Ok, but if she wants to know how it looks in those pants, what do I say?"

"Tell her her ass is perfect."

"THAT I can do!"

Her phone rings, and she sits up, dazed. It rings again, and she looks around. I watch silently as she pats the bed and asks herself in Italian where her phone is.

Hair messy. Makeup smeared. She looks radiant, but I know better than to grab the camera now and take a picture. She would freak out for sure. I answer, "It's on the nightstand on your left."

She looks at me like I have grown two heads, so I walk over and pick it up, then hand it to her. Finally, she focuses, then smiles a lazy, satisfied smile up at me, "Grazie, Mister Big Man. What time is it?"

After I tell her, I move away to get out of the storm's path. She blinks rapidly as she absorbs the news and logs it mentally into her appointment calendar. Then her eyes widen, and a look of sheer panic spreads across her face. She flings the covers off, begins rattling off in Italian how she is late for a gig, and sprints to the foyer where her clothes are. As she dresses, she calls her agent back and leaves a message that she's on her way. NOT to replace her.

I stroll in as she pulls her hair out from under her coat. She stops, eyeing my nakedness, then bounces up to me, puckering her lips.

"I must hurry, Americano, but thank you for that fottere of a lifetime." I place my lips on her waiting ones, and after the peck, she says, "Let me give you my digits. We can do this again, no?"

I'm silent. The moment of straight-line-no-curves truth is here. It won't do any good or ease the pain any less if I tell her she was an exceptional time and truly fun. So, I shoot her down. "No."

She stops, blinks rapidly, then backs up with a confused look on her hurried face. "No? You are saying no to me?"

"That's correct. There are no repeats. One night only."

"Uff!" She fusses incoherently in Italian as she exits the studio, slamming the door with force before she rushes down the stairs, cussing me the entire way.

I stroll out to the balcony to watch her race to her car. She stops on the sidewalk, looks up, shakes her fist at me, and screams a parting shot in perfect English. "You're an asshole!"

"No shit! Ciao, beautiful."

I tell the empty studio as I walk back in. "Well, that went better than usual," Picking up my camera, I remove the digital card and mark it #633, then walk through the bedroom to my editing station. Put it in the hard drive to upload later. Then walk back to the bed, and flop down on it. Pulling the pillows under my head, I grab my phone and call Darren.

"Thanks for calling me back." He answers immediately.

"What's up?"

"Remember my Frat brother who owns Been Jammin', the gentlemen's club in Vegas?"

"Refresh my memory."

"He bragged that he had discovered a dancer at Coyote Ugly, and she had turned out to be a gold mine. He made her his headliner and said she was his million-dollar baby. I told him if he came across another opportunity to give me a call." He pauses, "He called yesterday."

"I'm listening," I tell him.

"Her name is Seary, and she came to him a few months ago with an idea for a new niche service to provide customized sexual fantasies to his whales." He pauses for effect.

"I'm all ears now."

Darren chuckles, "Bart said anything this girl does makes money. She's like a money magnet, and a business guru all rolled into one. He says she is brilliant and has an intuitiveness that's impressive. I'm definitely interested in investing, and I thought you might be as well. But regardless if you do or don't, perhaps you have some insight on her."

"I don't frequent the gentlemen's clubs, so I haven't heard of her. But I know people who do. I can check her out for you. What are the investment details?" I put my feet on the floor and my elbows on my knees, listening to the offer as Darren discusses the deal. "Sounds like the investment is solid. When do you need an answer on the stripper?"

"Right away. He's gathering the initial capital investors now."

"Ok. I'm on Thanksgiving leave at the moment. I'll fly out and evaluate her. I need to check in on my properties anyway. Do you want me to check in with Bart while I'm there?"

"No. Just spy on her and give me your honest opinion on whether you think she's a winner."

"Affirmative. I'll let you know by the end of the week."

"Appreciate it."

"No problem. Ciao."

I hang up the phone and immediately begin texting my team.

Antonio:

> Change of plans. Charter a plane to Vegas as soon as possible.

Mia:

> I won't be coming by the office after all. Forward the contracts. I'll review and return them from here. Have you heard anything on the issue in North Dakota? Make sure we don't lose that bid. Also, I want to review the list of charities this year and the dollars allocated for each.

Adona:

> Cancel the remainder of the girls. I'm good for now.

Kip:

> I'll be flying into Vegas in the morning. What are the chances you can get us a couple of tickets into Been Jammin'?

Maria:

I'll be flying in tomorrow. Would sure appreciate it if I discovered some leftovers waiting for me in the refrigerator.

Adona responds first:

Is everything good?

Yes. Leaving Rome. No complaints. She was fun.

Good. I thought you would like her. She is still new to the business. A fresh face. Let me know when you need my services again. You know you are a special client.

Then Kip:

Text me when you're an hour out. I'll pick you up from the airport. Made reservations at the club. Looking forward to the show! Watching strippers never gets old.

Then Antonio:

You'll be flying JetAir. Leaving in two hours.

I update Angelo:

I'm flying out in two hours. Please pick me up AT MY APARTMENT IN 30.

Angelo answers:

Roger that, Boss. On my way now.

Maria sends:

Can't wait to see you! It's been too long. I'll have your favorite waiting. Safe travels.

And last, Mia answers. Her text is a chapter in a book, so I flip through it. Scanning it for anything that must be handled now. Nothing that can't wait until I'm in the air.

I head to the bathroom to shower and shave. Lathering up, I stroke my face with the razor and think about the concept of customized sexual fantasies. It is brilliant. Prostitution isn't legal in Vegas, but sex happens in the VIP rooms in the back. I smile at myself in the mirror.

I'm looking forward to learning more about this particular niche business.

I turn the shower on and step in. Sticking my head under the hot water, I close my eyes and think about nothing. Letting the wet warmth clear my mind and rejuvenate my body. When I step out, I dress in two layers. The first layer is for the heat in Vegas, and the outer layer is for the Italian chill. After grabbing a backpack, I lock up and trot down the stairs. When I emerge onto the street, Angelo is already waiting for me. On the way to the airport, we discuss the soccer match.

At the FBO, I say, "No need to park; just drop me off." When he stops, I thank him for the lift, shake his hand, grab my bag, and trot inside. I board the JetAir flight without incident. Once I'm strapped in, I pull out my laptop and begin reviewing the documents Mia sent over.

Halfway across the Atlantic, I finish, sign them, and hit send. Then I review the bid for the North Dakota fracking contract, verify the numbers are where they need to be, and give her the go-ahead to negotiate the terms.

Next, I review the list of charities and notice that Wounded Warriors isn't on the list. I send her a note to add them. I also remind her to make sure she sets up the scholarship for Bradford's children and pays off their home mortgage for his widow.

I close the laptop, take the pillow the flight attendant offers and settle in to catch up on my sleep.

"Please wake me when we are Stateside. I want to eat while the jet refuels."

"Yes, sir. Sleep well." He tells me as he pulls the shutters over the windows, blocking the sun.

I'm asleep before he finishes. ....

....

....

CHAPTER TWO

I'm driving to the flight line. Bradford sits next to me. Everett is in the back. Bradford is talking about his wife and kids. His youngest just started the first grade. Proud papa. He kisses his school picture and tucks it back inside his flight suit.

Everett unbuckles, leans up, and also shows off a picture of her kid.

Crack! Boom! The vehicle rocks nearly flips, then lands upright, hard, shaking us as it bounces to a stop.

My ears ring from the blast. All I can hear is the pounding of my heart in them, drowning everything else out.

The world shrinks. Time slows.

I survey the cab.

There's blood everywhere.

Bradford hangs dead in the passenger seat.

Anger floods my mind.

Rage drenches my body, mixing with the sweat in the heat of the Middle East.

Then ... a scream of deafening insanity.

The time returns to normal.

Everett is screaming.

I yell over her and command calm, "Soldier! Bow up!"

I move to help her. My harness is locked. The mechanism is jammed. I'm strapped to the seat. I try to rip it, but it's too strong.

My knife is in the lower side pocket of my flight suit. I stretch my arm down to the zipper. My fingers touch the edge of the metal, and nimbly, I gather the fabric, pushing the zipper open. I continue gathering more fabric until I touch the cold metal of my revolver. I flip the snap and pull it from its holster. Quickly cock it, and lay it across my lap. Then continue for my buck knife.

By the time I pull it from its sheath, there is complete silence. Only the deep, even, strained, heavy, controlled breathing of Everett fills the air. I glance back and receive an affirmative nod.

I cut the strap and free myself.

Lay my fingers on Bradford's neck, confirming his death. His jugular is quiet.

Exiting the vehicle, I quickly survey the area for danger and spot a burka running with a rifle. Knowing I must contain the situation if we are to get out of this alive.

Assessing the damage to the vehicle as I hurry to Everett's aid. I note: Roadside bomb. We are immobile. Trapped. Stranded. Alone.

I snatch hard on the damaged door to open it. Only the sound of heavy panting greets me as Everett forces control over the pain.

"Bradford?"

"Dead."

"Damn!"

Her leg is badly mangled. Blood has saturated the flight suit. I can't tell if it's an artery or a vein. I talk softly while I take my knife and cut the fabric off. "It's pretty bad, Easy, but you'll live."

Our eyes briefly connect as I unzip my flight suit and pull my arms out, letting it hang off my ass as I pull my t-shirt off. I cinch it tight. "Tourniquet. Just in case." I try to offer reassurance.

We both know she's a target. "Call it in and lay low. I'm going after the motherfucker. Shoot anyone who isn't wearing an American uniform. That's an order."

Everett nods. "Go."

I turn toward the closest building as I pull my flight suit back on, estimate the time that has ticked off, the distance to it, the time it will take me to run there, and whether the motherfucker is hiding inside. As I reach into my pocket to retrieve my weapon, I hear Everett say in a voice just above a whisper. "Hard, my gun is jammed."

Without hesitation, I hand mine over. "Here. Take mine. That's also an order."

I reach back in for my buck knife. As my fingers wrap around the handle, a feeling of calm fills me. All the years of hand-to-hand combat in our gladiator training with my cousin Augustus will give me the advantage. I just need to get my hands on them. I sprint to the building and hear the pride in his voice when I beat him for the first time. He dubbed me, The Bastard Son of Thor—a poke at my physical resemblance to Chris Hemsworth.

Entering the doorway, I slide quietly in. Checking the space for movement, listening with the intensity of a hunter. Knowing my prey is close but not knowing if I'll face off with a lone wolf or a pack, I stealthily move from room to room—every sense on high alert.

Climbing the steps to the second floor, I hear muffled voices from the top room. When I ease open the bedroom door, a shocking sight awaits. Two women are huddled together in the middle of the room with one, two ... six small children lying face down. Their tiny faces are hidden. Their little hands cover their ears. Only their sniffles can be heard. Along the wall to my right are three preteen boys standing at attention but shaking with fear. The whites of their eyes are clearly visible.

'Only a coward would hide here.'

"Shush." I raise my finger to my lips and begin to back out, pulling the door closed. As it swings, their focus shifts to what's hiding behind the door. Then sheer terror fills their faces in a split second, and an automatic weapon sprays bullets.

Instantly, the boys drop lifeless. Executed along the wall. Blood stains bear witness behind them. The women scream and drop to shield the children with their bodies. Wails fill the air.

I ram my body into the door, driving it back on the gunman, flattening him against the wall. Then snatch it off and attack with the thunder of my spirit and the ferocity of the roman heritage that pumps through my veins.

Hell-bent on securing not only Easy's safety and

the safety of the innocents writhing with terror on the floor but having my revenge for Bradford's death.

He fires the weapon haphazardly, trying to raise it to shoot me. My left hand chops his windpipe while my right stabs the knife to the hilt directly in the ball of his shoulder. The weapon's weight causes it to drop by his side, and he sprays harmless rounds into the floor.

I drive my body into his with crushing power, pinning him. A choke hold pinches off the scream of pain as I yank the knife out. Then I lift the enemy combatant off the floor like a raging bear, needing to look him in the eye. Blood soaks the burka disguise a deep red, and the sight is satisfying.

I stare ruthlessly at the choking red face of the murdering coward and see not a human but a demon staring back. The feeling of Bradford's lifeless jugular haunts me. Laying the edge of my buck knife's sharp blade against his neck, I slowly drag it across, using the edge of my thumb as a guide as my righteous eyes pierce his evil eyes.

As the blade sinks into his neck, I watch the evil turn into the fearful eyes of a mortal man who knows death has arrived to claim him. Then I slit his lifeline. Blood bursts forth with a velocity that shoots the ceiling, spraying it and painting it dark red.

Silence falls heavy, filling the room with a deafening void. I hold my attack until there is no life left, then I nimbly flip the knife through my fingers and return it to its sheath in my pocket. Its job is done. As I release the murderer, I take the automatic weapon from his lifeless grip, and his dead weight hits the floor with an echoing thud. I turn the weapon on the innocent occupants. No one is moving. Silent eyes stare at me.

My hard eyes stare back.

The only sound I hear is of my blood pounding and my calm breath inhaling and exhaling in rhythm with it.

When the soldiers burst into the room, the scene unfolds again as if in slow motion. They stand guard over the women and children, search the dead teen boys, give the all-clear signal, and escort the survivors from the room. The little ones' eyes pierce me to my core as they pass me: the pain, the fear, the unknown. When the women pass, their eyes are turned down as they approach, but one lost soul cuts hers at me, and I see their hopelessness.

Everett!

Rushing back down the stairs, real-time returns; I stop in the doorway just long enough to assess the current conditions outside and wipe the blood from my hands before I enter the light. Soldiers are everywhere, combing the area for more IEDs; and more enemy combatants. The situation is under control.

Making my way back to the vehicle, I arrive just as a medic exits. Looking in, I breathe a sigh of relief. My crew chief sits there smiling.

"You good, Easy?"

"Always," Everett says with a smirk and heavily glazed eyes. "Morphine is my new best friend, Hard."

I chuckle at that truth.

"Did you take care of business?"

"Always," I reply with the same smirk.

"Smart ass!" Then Everett's eyes clear, and they look directly into mine. "Did you find the son of a bitch?"

"Affirmative."

"Dead?"

"Yeah."

"Good!" She looks down at her mangled leg, then at the front seat where Bradford sat.

"Bradford?" I ask.

"He's been escorted back."

"Good." We stare at each other, knowing the pain of his death will bond us together forever. She opens her mouth to ask. I know she wants the details, so I

begin telling her before she has to."He was hiding as a woman."

"Piece of shit!" The venom in her voice is pure.

"Yeah. Hiding with the women and children."

"Are they okay?"

"He killed three boys before I could get my hands on him." She looks up. "Are you good?"

"Yeah." I smile at her, raise my arms and turn around so she can see I'm unscathed. "I'm good."

"How did you...."

"Knife," I answer before she can classify the killing, then hold my hand out. "My weapon, please."

She stares at my open hand, digesting the information and realizing I won't share any more details. She quietly lays the weapon in it. I check the safety, return it to its holster, and zip it up with the buck knife. "Looks like you'll be heading home now."

She looks down at her leg. "Yeah. Looks like a one-way ticket out of here." She takes a deep breath, then relaxes, letting the morphine have its way with her. When she looks up at me again, she says. "Easy Mama's going home to see my baby girl and my Badass Baby Daddy!"

The look on her face freezes my breath and tightens my gut. Wow!

She closes her eyes and drifts off to sleep, and I

stand there guarding her. When the medics return with a gurney, I wake her. "Easy. Time to go home." Her eyes flutter, and when she focuses on me, she smiles.

I continue standing guard over my friend as they remove her. When she passes me, she raises on one arm and holds her hand out. I walk over to clasp it.

"Take care of yourself, Easy. Your Badass Baby Daddy is one lucky man."

"Will do, Sir. You too." She grins, then laughs, falling back onto the gurney. "Yes, he is!" I watch momentarily, then walk away, knowing it's time to report to my commanding officer.

I hear her yell after me. "Hey, Hard? Don't stay that way." I throw my hand up, letting her know I heard her. "I'm serious, Asshole!" She yells.

That makes me laugh aloud, so I turn to face her but continue walking backward. "It's who I am." I grin and double-tap my heart with a closed fist. "Hard to the core." Then I spin around and continue walking away.

She yells again. "Don't forget hard head."

I sling both arms in the air, spin to face her again and give her a final middle finger salute, flipping her off.

"Affirmative. I won't forget you, Easy Mama."

"You better not!"

"I won't."

I can't.

....

....

....

The shutters in the cabin are lifted one by one, and the brightness brings me back to reality. I hear the flight attendant step up beside me, and I acknowledge I'm awake by lifting my hand. But I keep my eyes closed, wanting to stay in that moment for as long as possible before consciousness arrives and the memory blurs. As the vision that haunts me vanishes out of sight, my gut tightens, and I wonder...

Easy's face. Full of undeniable love.

It was unadulterated beauty.

Will I ever have someone who looks at me that way?

CHAPTER THREE

The plane touches down. Fully awake now, I brace myself for the momentum of the brakes. When the plane taxis down the runway, I pinch the bridge of my nose and let the raw emotions from the dream settle. Leaning my head back, pushing them down deep inside, not forgotten, but not harmfully harbored, I gain control of my psyche. They are a part of who I am now. I take a deep, cleansing breath.

I unbuckle and visit the restroom. When I return, my food has been served. The flight attendant stands by the seat, smiling at me. "Mr. Moore, what would you like to drink? Coffee? Water? Or perhaps something else? We have Crown Royal in the freezer."

That makes me smile. It's always nice when your preferred drink of choice is remembered. "I'm good with water. Thank you."

I spend the remainder of the flight to Vegas going over the architect's plans for the farmhouse in Alabama and making notes on the changes I want. About an hour out, I text Kip to let him know.

Las Vegas, NV

When the plane touches down, I'm caught up and ready to move forward.

Walking down the steps, I see Kip. He throws his hand up, and I wave back.

When I arrive at his car, he shakes my hand and slaps my back in a bro hug. "Aurelius, it's good to see you, brother." He takes my bag and throws it in the trunk.

"Likewise, buddy."

Kip is not only my real estate agent, but he's a

close friend. When I first began investing in the real estate market in Vegas, he was a fireman dabbling in real estate remodeling on his off days. Kip showed me his first 'fixer-upper,' and I negotiated with him to do my work. Since then, he has managed my portfolio, buying and flipping fixer-uppers, while his wife manages my rental units.

"Bianca sends her love."

"How's she doing?"

"Ornery as ever." Kip smiles.

"That's why you're still together. She doesn't take crap off you."

Kip laughs. "True dat. She's one tough little bitch."

I laugh, "Does she know you call her that?"

"Oh, hell no! And don't you go telling her either." He changes the subject. "So, do you want to do the house tour now, or do you want to go to your place first and rest? We'll head to Been Jammin' around midnight. If Surreal is performing, we don't want to miss her."

"I'm up for a tour now. I slept on the plane but want to return to the house to see the sunset. I'll meet you at Been Jammin'."

"Good deal. Let's start with the latest purchases, and we'll work our way down the list." Kip gives me the rundown as he drives. "This last batch of remodels is almost ready to flip. I think this team of subs is doing a better job than the last one. I have a group of fifteen houses I'm putting together to show to some Japanese investors." We spend the afternoon looking at properties, crisscrossing blocks, and suburbs.

When we've seen the last one, I ask him as he drives me back to my place. "Have you gone to Been Jammin' before?"

"Yeah. It's a happening place. Have you been yet?"

"No, I haven't. Tell me what you know about it."

"It's the hottest gentlemen's club in Vegas. I had to call in some favors to get us in tonight."

"Thanks for that. I appreciate it."

"I'm hoping we can catch a Surreal Show. They don't announce them ahead of time."

"I was wondering if you are familiar with the dancers?"

He cuts his eyes at me, and his eyebrows are raised. His voice is cautiously curious. "Somewhat. I'm not the regular I used to be since I hooked up with Bianca. She's coming tonight, by the way. She insisted." He laughs and mimics her voice, making me laugh. "'You'll be horny as hell within an hour, and no one's riding that hose but me.' But I know it's really to see you."

I crack up at that, knowing it's true and thankful it's open between us. Kip and Bianca are into BDSM and belong to a private club. She has been determined to get me to join them for a threesome for a long time now, but I ain't into that.

He chuckles. "She won't stop, you know."

I laugh. "I know, but it ain't happening."

He laughs now too. "I keep telling her that if you haven't already caved into her, you aren't going to, but she is a pitbull at heart."

I shake my head.

He goes back to my question. "Why do you ask about the dancers at Been Jammin'? Have you been referred to one?"

"Yes. Her name is Seary."

Kip whistles. "Dude. Nothing like shooting for the Star. Seary's the headliner there."

"Tell me everything you know about her."

"She's as hot as her name implies."

I wait, but he doesn't offer any more information. "That's all you know?"

"Well. Yeah. She's the Star. I don't have the pocketbook to know more than that."

I nod and look out the window, then after a few moments, I ask. "How much does she cost?"

Kip hits the brakes and slows down to a stop at the red light before he answers. He turns in the seat and looks me in the eye. "You're looking to score with her?"

"Maybe."

He grins, then takes off again. "I wish you luck, bro. I've never heard anyone talk about hitting that ho, but I know they do book her." He hits the blinker and pulls up to my house. "Are you sure you don't want to ride with us?"

"I'm sure. I'll meet you at the club."

"Ask for Beverly."

"Will do. Thanks for the tour. You're doing a great job."

He grins, gives me a head nod, and I walk around to the trunk to retrieve my bag. I hoist it out, then slam the trunk, double tap it, and he pulls away.

Walking up to my 4,000 plus square foot, four bedroom, four bath luxury house in the Red Rock Country Club Community in Summerlin, I wonder again why I bought such a big house when there is only me to live in it and part-time at that. I lay my thumb on the keypad at the security gate, again at the front door, and enter the quiet house.

Dropping the bag on the marble floor, my footsteps sound as I walk straight to the backyard to enjoy the magnificent view of the Red Rock sunset. Standing there watching the ball of fire dropping in the sky, I remember why I bought this big house. It has the most spectacular, breathtaking view of the setting sun, and I'm grateful again for my good fortune.

The motion sensor exterior security lights illuminate the green carpet of grass as I turn to go back to the house. The pool water has turned sapphire blue and provides a soft glow on the patio area. I strip, toss my clothes on a bench, take a deep breath, and dive in. Swimming underwater to the opposite side, I enjoy the peaceful silence, and the warmth is soothing. Surfacing, I fill my lungs full, toss my head to the side out of habit from my long hair days as a kid, and blow the water running down my face off my lips.

Knowing I have plenty of time, I dive back under the water, but surface to swim on top, letting my hands cut it like a knife as they enter, pulling my muscular frame, gliding effortlessly along, kicking only to keep my balance. At the end, I do a flip and push off to continue swimming nonstop. I stop at thirty complete laps, almost a half mile, and feel great.

Putting my hands on the pool's edge, I push up out of the water, throw my foot up and stand in the cold air. Goosebumps pop out, and I shake like a dog to expel the water, then grab my clothes off the bench and hurry back into the warmth of the house. Racing nothing but my cold nakedness, I run to the foyer to get my bag, tuck it under my arm like a football player, and sprint to the laundry room. The automatic motion sensors turn the lights on in each room as I go and turn them off as I leave. I drop my bag in front of the washing machine and find a folded towel on top, along with a pair of gym shorts and a note from Maria, my house sitter.

> "Aurelius, I know you didn't grab a towel from the pool house after your swim. It's too cold to be running around soaking wet, and put these shorts on. It's also too cold to be running around naked."

I smirk. She knows me too well.

> "Leftovers are in the refrigerator as requested. Let's do breakfast tomorrow and

catch up. Text me when you wake, and I'll come up to start cooking. Oh! And do NOT start laundry. I'll do it tomorrow. I mean it! Don't!"

I laugh at that and kick the bag to the wall out of the way, dry off with the towel, drape it over my shoulders, don the gym shorts, and head to the weight room.

As soon as I enter, I raise my arms and announce to the emptiness. "Pumping iron is good for the raging beast that lives within us." I work my way around the machines and finish in about 40 minutes. When I walk out, my muscles are swollen, and I'm confident I can handle anything that comes my way.

Heading into the kitchen, I open the fridge and stick my face inside. Umm. Homemade enchiladas!

I mix an after-workout protein shake and take it with me up the stairs to shower. Stepping under the water, I lather and think about my goal for tonight. I simply want to see Seary dance. If I like what I see, I'll book her and find out firsthand what her new business deal is about.

I hear Kip's voice again. She's as hot as her name implies. You're looking to score with her?

If she comes up with a customized sexual fantasy

that impresses me, I might let her work some magic on me. Hell, if she comes up with one I haven't thought of, I might invest in the new venture myself.

But then I hear Kip again, as he so poetically put it. I've never heard anyone talk about hitting that ho.

Why is that? Kip has eyes and ears all over Vegas. Someone would've talked about popping that princess. The thought that Bart could be scamming his Frat buddy makes me more determined to check her out. Darren's a good guy.

Turning the water off, I step out and decide to skip shaving. I'm on leave. No need to be smooth, but I splash aftershave on anyway. Then I go into the dressing room to choose my clothes for the evening.

Pressing the button, the closet doors slide inside the wall until my entire wardrobe is displayed. I picked a dark purple J-Crew shirt and dark distressed jeans. I'll blend in with the shadows and have a better opportunity to watch this dancer work. Walking back out, I push the button again, and the doors slide closed. Then I press the button below it, and the cabinet doors of the opposite wall slide back. My shoes rise in a stair-step display case. I pick a pair of black Converse sneakers and hit the button on my way out to close the cabinet. I dress in the bedroom. Stepping into my jeans, I'm thankful for Dilbert, my tailor, who customizes my clothes. The soft, distressed fabric sits snugly on my thighs and hugs my ass, but there is plenty of room in the crotch, so my balls aren't pinched. Putting my arms in the shirt sleeves, my biceps are tight in the fabric, and when I pull the shirt closed to button it, It's tight across my back. Hmm. Note to self. Call Dilbert. I need to be measured again. I've gained more muscle mass. I leave the top four buttons undone to accommodate my new size.

Opening the safe, I take enough cash to have a good time at the gaming tables if Seary is a dud and an open-limit credit card in case I lose my ass gambling early on. I have no intention of coming back to a lonely house before the sun rises. I fold the money around the credit card, slide the wad into a money clip, and then put it in my front pocket. Slipping into my shoes, I glance at my reflection in the mirror as I stand. I hear, "Mister, Very Big Man with the very big ass." True dat.

Trotting down the stairs, I head to the kitchen to heat Maria's famous enchiladas. While I eat, I catch up on the news, then wash my dishes. Walking across the house to the garage, my mood is light and carefree. I think I'll drive the Corvette. Sliding behind the wheel, I check the settings and the mirrors, then back out and circle the drive down to the security gate. Waiting for it to open, I tune the car's sound system to my playlist and turn it up. The speakers are booming with the bass.

Once I'm out on the open road, I push its limits. The car screams down the interstate. I love flying. An hour later, I'm heading back to Vegas and decide to visit Fremont Street.

CHAPTER

FOUR

It's alive with lights, music, sounds, and people milling around. Stopping at a red light, I see an Elvis street performer having his picture taken with a tourist, some young women with only body paint and g-strings on, and two nuns wearing habits that have their enormous, naked tits hanging out. I circle around, and at the next red light, I'm enjoying a Michael Jackson impersonator who is really good when I hear a TAP, TAP, TAP. I look out the passenger window and see a young woman smiling at me with her boobs about to fall out of her dress. I roll the window down, and she asks me. "Are you our Uber?"

Really? I'm in a Corvette. I laugh out loud and tell her, "No."

But she has stood up and is talking to her friend and doesn't hear me. Her hand is resting on the door in the open window. I lean over to communicate. She is giggling with her friend, and I realize they are very drunk. I also realize Vegas is not without predators, and she is putting them in danger, standing on the corner of Fremont Street asking strangers for lifts.

I make a command decision, reach over and pop the door open. Without hesitation, the giggling girl pulls it open. The interior lights come on, and I see a 6-inch-high stiletto heel enter the car first, then a heavy thigh, followed by a miniskirt stretched taut like a tent over a very curvy booty. She plops down in the passenger seat. Her sweater top has a scoop neck, and she has it pulled down too low. Her breasts are bulging out of the top. She doesn't look at me but rather prepares to receive her thin friend. The skinny one backs in, sitting on her lap. She tucks her knees up under her chin and swings around to face front. Their drunken giggles fill the small space as she attempts to close the heavy door car.

The traffic light turns green. The car behind us honks. The door isn't shut.

I lean over and stick my arm between them. "Here. Let me get that for you."

When my hand moves theirs aside and grasps the

door handle, both of them stop moving and quit giggling. They watch as I pull the door firmly shut, then turn to look at me. I smile and ask, "Where to, ladies?"

The curvy one's jaw literally falls open, and the skinny one's eyes nearly bug out of her thin face. The interior light dims as I pull away, and the cab goes dark. They burst into mad giggling again, then whisper as if I can't hear them.

"Holy hell! What a hottie!"

"His eyes. Did you see his eyes?"

I ask again, "Where to ladies?" Cutting my eyes for an answer, they are both staring at me as if I was a celebrity and I can't but laugh.

Then the curvy girl answers. "Excalibur."

"Cool." I introduce myself. "I'm Aurelius Moore."

The skinny girl speaks first. "Hi. I'm Stella." She turns a pretty shade of pink, and I can tell right away that Stella is not as drunk as I first thought but very shy.

"Hi. I'm Nina." The girl on the bottom introduces herself and pokes Stella.

"Are you ladies here celebrating something?"

Stella pushes her glasses up her nose. "Graduation."

Graduation? I cut my eyes at them again. Are

they 21? They look a lot younger. Surely they are college graduates and not high school. "Where did you go to college?"

"USC." Nina offers without missing a beat. Damn. They must be 21. I look over again, sizing them up, and feel ... a lot older. It must be my tours of duty.

"First time to Vegas?"

"Yeah!"

"First day?"

"Yeah!" They giggle again.

"What are you girls going to see at the Excalibur? The Tournament of Kings?"

They laugh and high-five each other. "No. The Thunder From Down Under."

"Of course," I smirk. Where else would two young girls, needing to blow off steam on their first night in Vegas, want to go?

Stella leans down to hear what Nina whispers, and she answers. "Right? That would be so fly!"

Their eyes stare at me. Gawk actually. I reach over to adjust the temperature. "Is it warm enough for you?"

Stella says. "Oh yes. I'm really warm."

"I'm getting downright hot," Nina says, then

bursts into a new round of drunken giggles and Stella can't help but join her.

It's infectious, and I chuckle too.

As soon as it gets quiet, they resume their gawking again, and it's awkward. I keep my eyes on the road and try to keep the conversation from going any further south. "What did you major in?"

Nina answers. "I majored in education."

"A teacher, then."

"I bet I could teach you a thing or too." She says under her breath.

I ask Stella. "And you? Are you a teacher too?"

Nina snorts and I look at them. "No, she majored in...."

Stella cuts her eyes at Nina, shooting darts, and fills in the answer. "Security. I majored in security."

I can't hide my surprise with that answer. This girl weighs all of 100 pounds. "Security? Really? You don't look like a badass."

A smirk plays on her lips. She is trying hard not to join her giggling friend. "It's I.T. security."

"Are you a hacker?" I look back at the road.

Nina snorts again. "Sort of. It's in social engineering." I cut my eyes at them. Now they have my attention.

"Social engineering? What's that?" I play dumb.

Stella looks out the window and answers with a straight face. "I find and prevent perps from screwing corporate accounts." She doesn't take her eye off the sights outside.

"Hmm. I've heard they can infiltrate and hold servers hostage. Is that true?"

She looks surprised at me. "Yes. Absolutely and some bad hackers demanded ransoms!"

"How do you find these bad guys?"

Nina burst out laughing again, and we both look at her. "She performs penetration tests. HAHAHAHA!"

I can't help but laugh with her, and Stella smiles when I ask, "Really? What kind of penetration tests?"

She clears her throat and tries valiantly to be professional. "I'm a white hat."

Nina can't help herself. She leans on the door and cackles, making me chuckle with her again.

Stella manages to remain serious. "Do you know what that is?"

"I do." I smile and wink.

Nina comes up for air and blurts. "My best friend is a virtual corporate condom." Then she snorts again and gives in to the giggles.

Stella laughs with us and tells me. "Wait for it. She's not finished."

"She's going to be going down on all the big dickheads too. HAHAHAHA! That's sooooo fuuuucking fuuuuuunny!"

We enjoy a good laugh as I maneuver to the curb outside Excalibur. "We have arrived, Ladies."

Nina starts wiping her eyes and getting her giggles under control.

"The men from the Outback await you. I hope you enjoyed your ride." I lean over and pop the door open for them. Stella twists in the tight space and holds her phone up, "Mind if we Snapchat?"

I grin, "I don't mind."

They do their thing. I give them a thumbs-up and a nice smile, then Stella gets out. Nina puts her feet on the sidewalk and tries to rise. "Oh no! I'm stuck." She bursts out laughing again. "Stell, give me a hand."

She does, and Nina grasps it and does her best to lift her ass up while Stella leans back, pulling as hard as she can, but it's not enough. Nina is stuck. She lets go of Stella's hand, and Stella stumbles backward, trying not to fall. Nina has another fit of giggles, and I know she won't be able to get out as long as she's laughing. So I lean over, put my mouth right next to her ear, and drop my voice to a very deep tone, giving her a taste of seduction. "Baby Girl. You're gonna need some big strong hands to help."

Her laughter dies immediately. She freezes, listening. My voice stays low.

"The problem with 6" heels in a sports car that's only 15" off the road is the center of gravity shifts."

She turns her head and looks me in the eye. I can smell the liquor on her breath.

"I can help you if you want."

"What do you suggest?" Her voice is breathless.

"You can take your shoes off and climb out on your own, or I can give you a push."

"What kind of push?" She smirks, flirting.

"The kind that you will remember for the rest of your life."

She grins and says. "I'm down for that."

I grin back. "Good Girl. Lean up as far as you can."

She does as instructed. I place my hands on her waist, rubbing her with my thumbs to relax her. I then slide my fingertips down her curves, forcing them between her miniskirt and the leather of the car seat. Cupping her ass and squeezing her as I go, I inch my fingers down. When they leave the miniskirt behind and touch her bare skin, she says in a voice that shows she is thrilled she chose this method. "Oh, my!"

"You're so hot!" I whisper in her ear as they inch further under her into heaving position. When her ass is sitting on my hands and part of my forearms, I ask, "Ready, Baby?"

"Yes." Her voice is full of anticipation.

"Ok. Here's what I want you to do for me," I whisper in her ear. I see Stella's shoes come into view, but Nina waves her away. "On the count of three, I'm going to thrust my hands up, and I want you to enjoy it, arching your back and pushing those beautiful breasts of yours up to the stars."

"Oh, my!" She says again.

"Can you do that?"

"Yes." She takes a deep breath, "I can do that."

"Ok. Here we go." I lay my lips on her ear and breathe into it, then I whisper. "One. Two." I blow in it while I grip her ass firmly, curling my fingertips into her skin.

"Oh, my goodness!" She says, with a voice that tells me my fingers are pulling her slit open.

"Three," I tell her with a commanding voice while I heave her ass up. She arches her back, pushes her boobs to the stars, and her ass lifts out of the seat smoothly. Then I push her from the car.

For a moment, she rocks on her heels, then staggers forward a little until she gains control of the momentum. Then she burst into a fit of giggles again and jumps up and down, asking Stella. "Did you get that? Did you get it? Please! For God's sake! Tell me you got it."

Stella holds up the phone and says. "I did! I did! Calm down. You're gonna break your heels." Nina snatches the phone from her friend and begins to watch the replay, while Stella sticks her head in the car. Pushing her glasses up, she tells me, "We appreciate the ride."

"You betcha." I reach for a business card. "You do realize I'm not an Uber, right?"

She grins. "Yeah. It was a dare."

"Ah!" I laugh and hand my card to her.

She takes it, reads it, then smiles. "Maximus Enterprises, huh?"

I nod. "When you get home, look me up. I could use your skills."

Her smile is radiant. "I will. Thanks." Then she closes the door.

I check the traffic, then I hear TAP, TAP, TAP. I put the window down.

Nina sticks her head inside, grinning from ear to ear. "Thanks for the lift."

"No problem," I give her a wink.

"I'll never forget it."

I grin, knowing she won't. "You ladies enjoy the Thunder From Down Under show."

"You dancing tonight?" Her giggles return.

I chuckle and shake my head. "No."

"Too bad. I was going to return the favor." She curls her fingers in a claw, and I laugh out loud. Then she makes a fist and shoves it at me. "Hashtag Hottest Uber Ever!"

I give her a knuckle bump. "You girls, stay safe."

As I pull away, I hear her tell Stella. "Damn awesome dare, Stell!"

CHAPTER

FIVE

Been Jammin' is down the strip from the Excalibur. When I pull in, I drive under the canopy and wait my turn for valet parking. An older man takes my information, then takes my car. When I enter the building, I notice several things. One, like all the other casinos, there are a lot of people coming and going, but unlike the others, there isn't a hotel associated with it. When you enter Been Jammin', you step immediately into the casino area, and the sounds of the slot machines hit you. They have their own distinct music. Each time I hear it, I know I'm home.

I find the sign that says Gentleman's Club, and I head that way, taking my time and enjoying my stroll. Deeper into the casino, I hear "Wheel of Fortune" and the click, click, click of a simulated wheel turning, then someone squeals.

They've hit the jackpot. Passing the gambling tables, I stop and take my time to study the limits and dealers. Walking around the whole area, knowing if I'm going to play, I want to find the right fit. I need to find a dealer who is engaging the table. Most of the dealers are stiff and polite, but across the area, I can see a crowd around one, so I head that way. When I get close enough, I stop and observe a redhead in a tight, black corset with beautiful plumpness overflowing and nice plump buttocks. She has a full table of gamblers. Laughing as she deals, the whole table cheers. People are stopping to watch. She's the one. I'll come back to her table.

Turning away, I again locate the sign pointing to the Gentleman's Club. I pass several stores selling merchandise. The aroma smells good when I pass the Steakhouse Restaurant and decide to eat breakfast there.

I take my phone out and text Maria.

Better make our date lunch.

OKAY. :(

I smile at the phone and return it to my pocket. She's the best.

When I arrive at the Gentleman's Club, the atmosphere is set with a small patio-style area outside the triple set of entrance doors. Cocktail tables with simple straight-back chairs are placed inside the railing, and waitresses clad in nothing more than pasties and G-strings comb the area serving drinks. It's packed, and the sound of conversation buzzes over the piped music from inside. At the gate in the railing, there are two hostesses working the podium. I walk over, and they greet me with pleasant smiles. "Good evening, Sir. How may we serve you?"

"Good evening, ladies. I'm looking for Beverly."

"She's inside. Is she expecting you?"

"Later in the evening."

"I can text her someone is waiting to see her if you like?"

"Thank you."

"Sure." She takes her phone. "Who may I say is here?"

"Aurelius Moore."

Her eyebrows flinch, telling me she wasn't expecting Aurelius, then she begins texting. The other hostess asks me. "May we offer you a drink while you wait?"

"That would be nice. I'll have Crown neat, please."

She also takes her phone and sends a text.

"Beverly will be right out."

I nod and step back to let another patron approach. While I wait, I examine the banners hanging from the rafters over the area. All of them are advertising a dancer named Surreal, but they appear to be Brittney Spears, Jennifer Lopez, Katy Perry, and other famous celebrities. In the center is the only one that has an unknown dancer. Her face is covered by a bejeweled black and gold Mardi Gras mask. The banner shows her on a stripper pole doing a full split, gripping it between her legs. Her arms push her large round breasts out of an open heart-shaped hole.

She is HOT! I thought Seary was the headliner, but this Surreal is definitely the star attraction.

When I turn back to the hostess podium to ask, I almost knock my drink out of the hands of a nice-looking woman dressed in a red sequined gown. My reflexes catch the glass and stabilize it in her hands. She is unfazed, smiling, and introduces herself. "Mr.

Moore, I'm Beverly. Welcome to Been Jammin'. How may I assist you?"

"I'm going to gamble at table #56. I would appreciate a call when my party arrives."

"Certainly. I will see to it personally. Have you enjoyed our tables before?"

"No. I can't say that I have."

"Well, allow me to register you so you won't have to cash out your chips."

"I appreciate that."

"This way." She turns, and I follow as she steps around the patio area and enters a black side door with a key code that is next to invisible to the naked eye. We step into a plush hallway with doors leading off each side. A showgirl enters with an older gentleman in tow. She escorts him into one of the side doors and closes it.

Beverly explains. "This area is reserved for our VIP members. I would be happy to schedule a tour. My office is right here." She opens the door and waves me inside.

I enter to find a large office with a desk at one end. A couch and two sitting chairs frame a coffee table at the other. There are autographed pictures of her with a who's who of icons in the entertainment industry. The celebrities vary from Wayne Newton to Justin Bieber. I step up to the wall and begin scanning all the pictures. While she walks to her desk, takes the laptop off, and sits on the couch. "Let's get you hooked up."

I smile at her words, then dig my money clip out of my pocket, unwrap the credit card, and hand it to her with a smile.

She smiles back, closes her computer, stands and takes the card, then walks back to her desk while I sit down and enjoy the drink she brought me. I ask her my questions while watching her scan it, knowing it will answer all her questions.

"Who is Surreal?"

She glances up. "She's our star performer."

"Who is Seary?"

"She's our headliner."

She opens a drawer and takes a card out, and activates it. "How much are your VIP rooms?"

"That's between you and your choice from our talented dancers." She smiles and hands me both cards. "Present our card whenever you are here in the club. It will be all you need."

I stand and return them to my pants pocket. "Thanks." Bending back down to pick up my unfinished drink, I ask. "What's the difference between being a star and being a headliner? Besides the money."

She laughs as she shows me out the way we came in. "One is an entertainer, and one is a stripper." I eye the door at the end of the hall, but it is quiet, and I realize the rooms are completely soundproof.

When she shows me through the hidden side door, I ask. "May I access this door with my card? I'm a very private man."

She shakes her head. "I'm afraid not. All customers must use the nightclub to enter. I'm sure you understand."

She pulls the door closed, ensuring it is locked, then smiles at me and says. "It was a pleasure meeting you. I'll send you a notification when your party arrives. Our staff will take good care of you. If you need my assistance, you need only ask."

"I appreciate your time tonight, Beverly. Thank you."

She tilts her head and nods. "It was my pleasure. Rebecca is working table #56. She'll be expecting you." I give her the same tilting head nod, then walk away. She calls after me. "Good luck. I'll see you again at midnight."

I raise my hand, acknowledging I heard her.

When I arrive at Rebecca's table, there is still a

crowd surrounding it and the same five people gambling. Two of them are laughing, and three of them are not, but all of them have a nice stack of chips. Rebecca looks up and says to me. "Mr. Moore. It's good to see you."

I grin, "Likewise, Rebecca."

She smiles and deals another round to the table. She asks as she waits for them to give her direction. "Will you be playing with me tonight?"

Was that an innuendo?

I chuckle, "Perhaps I will get lucky."

She drops her eyes and grins as she makes her way down the five players with another card. The three who weren't grinning upon my arrival take a hit and bust their hands before she shows her card. The first two stayed, and she flips her card to reveal blackjack. Everyone groans, and she leans forward to collect their chips, giving everyone an ample view of her cleavage.

When she stands back up, I ask her. "How long are you working tonight?"

"Until dawn." She tells me while she deals another round.

The first two players take a hit and stay at 17. The next two are at 19. Everyone is smiling. The last one takes a hit and wins with 21. Rebecca turns her card over to reveal she has a Queen and a ten. They groan again. The player on the end looks at me and says, "You can have my spot, bro. Her luck is changing."

I sit down and hand her my new Been Jammin' card. She swipes it, then slides it back with a large stack of chips. The eyes of the others gamblers are on us. I peel two off the top and push them back to her. She accepts the tip graciously, then turns her attention back to the entire table and says, "Place your bets."

I put four chips in the betting circle and watch her manicured hands deal the cards. I can tell by the way she handles the deck that she has been a dealer for years. I sit in silence, playing each round and paying attention to the cards as they pass through the deck. I'm not an accomplished card counter, but I'm not unskilled when it comes to blackjack, either.

As it turns out, I do win more chips than I lose. After an hour, the original gamblers have all left, and before others take their place, I question her.

"How long have you worked here?" I push my chips to place my bet.

"Three years."

"Have you always been a dealer?"

"No. I began as a dancer." She deals the hand.

"Why aren't you dancing now?"

She smiles. "Better hours and less work."

"Ah!" I fall silent and tap the table to take a hit. She flips a queen up, and I bust. I lean back and stretch my arms as she grabs my chips, enjoying the view. A cocktail waitress stops beside me and asks if I would like a drink. I order my usual, then ask Rebecca as I bet again.

"So, who is Surreal?"

"She's our star attraction."

"Is she any good?"

She smirks at me, raises an eyebrow, and repeats her statement. "She's our Star attraction!"

I laugh. "I saw her banner. She must be outstanding."

"She's our ...."

I hold my hand up and stop her, laughing with her. "Did you dance with her?"

"I did."

"What can you tell me about her?"

"Nothing."

I tip my head and say, "Now, come on."

She laughs. "I'm not at liberty to discuss her."

I slide six chips her way and raise my eyebrows with a smirk.

She takes the chips. "Thank you. That's very generous of you."

"I just want to know how good she is."

She eyes me. "Are you a reporter, a blogger, or ?" She stops short of accusing me.

"A stalker?" I laugh at that. "Do I look like a stalker?"

She stays serious. "No, but a girl can't be too careful. Why are you asking?"

"It's business, not personal."

She studies me. "An agent?"

"An investor."

"Ah!" She says, knowing that's the truth.

I stand up, pull my money clip out, and find a business card to give her.

She looks at it and says, "She's the STAR attraction because she is unbelievably awesome at what she does."

I chuckle, "Is that the only answer I'm going to get out of you?"

She grins, then says, "I truly can't tell you anything other than that."

The cocktail waitress returns, and I tip her, then ask, "Who is Surreal?"

She answers the same way. "She's our star attraction."

"Can you tell me anything else about her?"

She says, "No. Top secret." Then walks away to deliver the other drinks on her tray.

I look back to Rebecca for clarification. "Her identity is top secret?"

She looks at me with a confused grin. "Yes."

"But you danced with her?"

"Yes, I did. It was very stressful. Some of the celebrities are absolute bitches. A screw-up or misstep might mean your career, you know?"

She looks at me, wanting me to agree, but the confused frown on my face makes her laugh. "No. You obviously don't know."

"I'm confused. What am I missing here?"

"When there is a 'Surreal' performance," she quotes with her fingers, "No one knows if the dancer is Surreal or J- Lo, or Brittany, or Beyoncé."

"Oh! She's an impersonator!" I laugh. "I missed that key fact."

"She's an excellent investment if that is what you want to know."

A new player sits down, and our conversation ends for several games. Then I ask her, "So, do you miss dancing?"

"Not really." The other player stands, "I enjoy dealing, and the tips can be just as good." She smiles at him. He smiles back and slides her a chip. She thanks him, and he leaves. She deals another game to me.

"What can you tell me about Seary?" I ask for a hit by touching my cards.

She smirks as she flips one up for me. "She's our headliner."

I smirk back and cover my cards. "Did you dance with her too?"

"Yes. I did, and she's the real reason why you're asking these questions."

I laugh, "Busted. Tell me about her." Leaning forward, I rest my forearms on the table and study her. "Is she any good?"

She laughs, "She's our headliner. Of course, she is good." She takes two cards and loses.

When she pushes my winnings to me, I ask, "Can you talk about her?"

"Yes. I can talk all day about her."

"So talk." I tip her two chips, then push four more at her. She eyes them, and I lay my hand down on top of them, covering them. "Tell me everything you know about Seary."

She laughs out loud. "She's great! The best dancer I've ever had the pleasure of sharing the stage with."

"What makes her so special?"

"Special? She's not just special. She's unforgettable."

I laugh at that over-the-top analysis, and she says, "I'm serious. She is more than a natural talent. She's a phenom."

I smirk, and she gets defensive. "I'm telling you straight up. Her dance interpretation is so unique!" She looks away, remembering. "It's really amazing the way she lets go, getting into the music and the moment. There is no counting, no thinking, just pure art." She looks back. "Seary is one of those dancers that comes along once in a lifetime. You'll get to see her tonight. She's scheduled to dance."

I nod. "I'm looking forward to it. Anything else you want to add?" I look down at the chips under my hand.

She grins really big. "Yeah. She's a real sweetheart too. The kind of girl that other girls love." Her fingers touch her ear, and she looks down at the table, then smiles a bright smile. "Your party has arrived and is waiting for you with Beverly."

"Excellent," I push the chips to her and stand. "Thanks for the intel."

"No problem. Stop back by on your way out later."

"If you're still here, I will," I wink at her.

"I want to hear you say. 'Rebecca. You were right. Seary is unforgettable.'"

I chuckle and give her a doubtful smile. "It takes a lot to impress me." Then I turn and walk away to find out for myself.

CHAPTER SIX

Siri Wright
Stage name: Seary

"Baby Girl, we have a birthday boy in the audience." My stage manager James walks over to my costumes and flips through them absentmindedly. "Do you want to start with him? Or do him later? I'm going to let Red and Lola do the honors tonight." He whirls around for my answer.

"Let's do him first. Get the crowd involved early." I turn to look at him as he walks over to me.

"What do you think about throwing in a Surreal performance halfway through tonight?"

"Well," he runs his fingers through my hair, "That depends on which one."

"I feel like being Beyoncé tonight. How about 'Dance For You?'"

He smooths my hair while he thinks, then he spins around and heads out the door. "Yes, we can do that. I'll set it up."

Cat comes in before the door closes. "Are you doing a Surreal performance tonight?"

I laugh. "Does James have his game face on?"

She nods as she comes in. "Which one?"

"The first one." I look at her in the mirror as she stands next to me. "I'm nostalgic tonight."

"Good nostalgic or bad nostalgic?"

I laugh. "Good nostalgic. I had a nightmare about being an accountant, and I was reminded I live a life others only dream of."

She leans down to give me a hug and a kiss on the cheek. "Let me go tell Bart, so he can contact Beyoncé's agent."

At the door, she says, "How about you and me taking a spa day on Friday? We haven't hung out as just friends in forever."

"I would like that." I smile at my manager, mentor, and best friend.

Aurelius

Walking up to the entrance of Been Jammin', I see Bianca and Kip with their arms around each other. They make a striking pair. He is all of 6'5" and 280 pounds of pumped-up mass, and she is all of 5'8" and 180 pounds of tough stuff. She likes to refer to herself as fluffy, but there isn't anything fluffy about her. She is tattooed, with half a mohawk and piercings that shout alternative lifestyle. Since I hired her to manage my rental properties, uncollected rents, and turnovers have dropped significantly.

When she sees me, she squeals and runs to me. I brace myself for impact, and she jumps into my arms, giving me a big crushing hug and saying in her sweet, high-pitched, fluffy voice. "You handsome Asshole! I've missed you!"

I look over her head at Kip, and he's smiling from ear to ear. I ask her as she drops off my body, and I spank her rear. "Sup, Tough Stuff?"

"You are looking so fly!" She says and hugs me. "I so desperately needed this date night with my men. Thank you, Baby."

We walk arm and arm back to Kip, and I shake hands with him while Bianca puts herself between us and hooks her thumbs in our belt loops, letting everyone know that we are both with her tonight and off limits. The two hostesses I met before are eyeing us, but Beverly is cool and professional as she walks up.

"Your table is ready. I'll escort you inside."

I motion for Bianca to go first, but she pushes me to follow Beverly, then her hand slips into mine. Looking back, she grins wickedly while she pulls Kip after her.

When we stop at the entrance door and wait our turn to go through, Beverly asks. "Did you enjoy Rebecca?"

"I did. I had a good time with her."

Bianca squeezes my hand hard, and I frown down at her.

She asks in a hiss rather than a whisper, "Who the hell is Rebecca?"

I glance at Kip for help. He pulls Bianca to him and kisses the top of her head while I answer, "Blackjack dealer."

Her eyes are narrow when she mouths silently to me, "Better be."

I laugh at her possessiveness and turn back to Beverly. She leads us into the club, and I'm amazed at the size. Quickly getting my bearings, I analyze the floor plan and realize multiple clubs are inside. This first one is as big as a concert hall and houses numerous bars, dance floors, and a big stage along one wall, with the other walls decorated with live dancers inside cages.

Beverly proceeds straight through to the sign that reads, "Gentleman's Club." It is also big, with multiple bars and a stage on one wall, but instead of floor space for dancing, there are cocktail tables with a maze of runways with stripper poles.

When Beverly stops, we are at the table at the end of the main runway. "Best seats in the house. Enjoy the show." She states, then walks away.

Our waitress takes our order, then vanishes. The three of us sit facing the stage. Bianca, naturally in the middle, puts both elbows on the table, folders her fingers, and rests her chin on her thumbs. She watches the dancer right before us, twirling around the pole.

Kip looks at me and nods in her direction with a 'check out her intensity' look, and I grin back at him. The dancer has some seriously sexy moves, and pole dancing will be on Bianca's To Do list next week, no doubt.

Surveying the room as the music thumps hard enough to feel, I see at minimum twenty dancers twirling around us on the poles or bumping and grinding on the runways, and maybe another ten offering lap dances on patrons in the audience. Keeping my eyes averted from the sensual dance happening right in front of our table so my bulge doesn't grow any larger, I notice a few girls leading customers off, and I can only assume they are heading to the VIP rooms for a private dance.

Suddenly the whole place literally thumps once with a deafening bass and strobe light. Then the room goes completely black. Startled, Bianca makes a small yip and sits back in her chair. The room is quiet for a split second, then THUMP, THUMP. THUMP, THUMP.

Scanning the room during the strobe flashes, I see that all the dancers are heading out. In silence,

Kip leans over to me and says. "Perfect timing. Seary is about to perform."

I lean over to him. "I certainly hope she's as good as all the hype."

THUMP, THUMP. THUMP, THUMP... THUMP, THUMP. THUMP, THUMP.

The timing is a heartbeat. Nice!

The heartbeat THUMP matches the song cadence as "Sex" by Cheat Codes & Kriss Kross Amsterdam plays. In the strobes, I see ten dancers in only G-strings and pasties pairing up and posing in different sexual positions, then dancing and rearranging their pairs.

Kama Sutra, sweet.

There is one dancer who seems to be the main attraction. I analyze her quickly. She is blonde, yes, and has a great body, including big breasts and a nice ass, but she isn't what I was hoping for. She is outstanding, and her dance skills are superb but forgettable.

Our waitress comes up with our drinks and leans over me to place them on the table. Bianca, back in charge, leans forward and practically hisses at her. She smiles at me nonetheless, and I can't help smiling back. I straighten my leg and reach in my pants pocket, pull off a couple of bills and tip her g-string. She grins and leans down to talk in my ear. "I'll be back to check on you, big boy, in a little while."

I nod, and she disappears. When I look back at the table, Bianca is glaring at me. "What?" I say innocently and reach for my drink.

I can see her mouth moving, but because of the loud music, I thankfully can't hear a word. Kip is clueless. His eyes are feasting on the dancers.

Taking a sip of Crown, I nod my head at Kip. She looks over at him and realizes she isn't the center of his universe at the moment, and she turns her attention back to him. Holding my drink in my lap, I concentrate on enjoying the show.

As the song ends, the dancers lay lengthwise on the stage, head to head and toes to toes, in a single line, and the big-breasted girl, I assume is Seary, crawls over them. Dragging her hair over their abs, she tosses her mane, making it whip them while she twerks. The site is sexy as hell as she moves down the line.

Whoever thought that up knows how to insight arousal.

The dancer reaches the end and splays out too. The thumping gradually gets softer and softer while the stage and runways slowly illuminate, dimming the effects of the strobes still matching the bass.

I look at Kip and Bianca. She slid closer to him and hooked his arm so her breasts push into it. I smile, lean forward and say, "That was hot!"

"Yeah, it was." Kip agrees.

Bianca reaches for her drink. "It was a good warm-up for Seary."

"That wasn't Seary?"

"Hell, no!" Kip exclaims. "That's the opening act."

"Oh, I didn't realize that."

Bianca grins over her drink and winks at me. "Get ready to get horny, Baby."

I look back at the stage and take a sip of Crown. Someone has placed a straight-back chair on it, and two dancers with flamingo feathers stand beside it.

The voice of an announcer booms in the room. "We have a birthday boy in the house. Johnny Robinson, please stand up."

The crowd erupts with cheers and clapping as a young man at the table next to ours stands. The announcer continues as the dancers carry the chair down the runway to where he stands. "Johnny is twenty-one!" More cheers and clapping. "You know what that means!" Chants of "Seary's Hot Chair" start, and the announcer says. "Johnny ... if you dare ... take Seary's Hot Chair."

The THUMP, THUMP, THUMP, and the strobes return with a different rhythm. Johnny, whose grin is from ear to ear, waves again to everyone, but he shakes his head, declines the dare, and sits back down at his table.

The crowd yells, "Take the chair! Take the chair!"

Kip leans toward him, cups his hands beside his mouth, and chimes in. "Yo, Johnny boy! Take the fucking chair, Brother!"

Bianca rolls her eyes. She leans over and tells me, "He wishes it was him."

Johnny's friends pull him from his chair and push him onto the stage. The two strippers take him by the arms and guide him to his birthday throne. Before he sits, he flips everyone off, and the crowd roars with laughter. Then he plops down in the chair and finds himself promptly tied to it. He leans his head back, and I can see the dread in his body language.

The lights go dark again, except for the beam of a direct spotlight on him and one circling the curtain on the stage. The crowd goes instantly silent as the THUMP, THUMP, THUMP, and strobes take over. Anticipation is heavy in the air. The tension is thick as the excitement builds, then the plucked notes of an electric guitar fill the room, and I recognize "So Contagious" by Acceptance.

Hmm. Interesting choice. Not what I was expecting for a lap dance.

Kip leans over and shouts, "This will be good."

But I don't hear him. The circling spotlight found its target when the curtain was pulled back, and a goddess dances onto the stage. I know, without a doubt, this is Seary!

CHAPTER
SEVEN

Staring at her, spellbound by her beauty, my mind goes blank. My hand hunkers down on my drink, and I struggle to get a grip on myself. Undeniable lust bursts forth within me.

Wow! This is unexpected!

She boldly bounces onto the stage to perform for a crowd of drunken fools, but her graceful movement belies her occupation, and I recognize a gifted and talented dancer before me. She moves with the elegance and poise of someone who could, and probably should, be dancing on a larger, grander scale. She is perfection in motion.

I sit motionless, completely spellbound, and locked down tight in my seat, not wanting to miss a thing. Appreciating that every moving part of her beautiful body is in total rhythm with the beat. Right down to the slightest nuance of the melody. She is incredible.

Her costume, or rather the lack of it, is breathtaking in its simplicity. She is not wearing a single piece of cloth, but rather she is wrapped in small gold chains. Her skin tone is healthy and natural. Not a fake salon tan, but sun-kissed with a faint tint of red. Her tan accentuates the gold chains that reflect the light from the intense spotlight, highlighting her voluptuous body. As she moves and flows, dancing toward me and heading to Johnny, her breasts stir my lust even further. They are perfectly proportioned and symmetrical, but they are moving and flowing, bouncing up and down, jiggling out the top of a gold bodice. My tongue touches a corner of my lips and plays there. The thought of taking soft, little pieces of her velvety skin between my lips, to run tongue against her, tasting her, then grazing her with my teeth, nipping her, makes my blood surge with desire.

Little gold chains are wrapped around her long graceful neck, and her platinum blonde hair is drawn high in a ponytail that sways from side to side with each strut, held in place by a single gold ribbon. A gold chain G-string and gold stilettos complete her costume. As she mixes her dancing between erotic and exotic, her body glitters.

When your body is that perfect, there are no flaws to hide.

I'm unable to take my eyes off her, unable to see anything else, and unable to hear anything but the music of her dance as her body literally sings like a siren to me. No woman has ever had this effect on me.

She is simply stunning!

When she reaches Johnny, she begins to twirl faster and faster, unspooling the first layer of gold chains, slowly revealing more and more of her beautiful, flawless skin. When she stops abruptly, her breasts are barely covered, and they rebound from the velocity in a sexy rolling motion as they come to rest in their proper place.

She is stacked and packed.

She pulls off the gold ribbon holding her hair and shakes her blonde mane out, letting it float like a cloud down around her shoulders. Then she takes the ribbon and twirls it, making it float in the air as she dances under it. Doing a couple of spinning hair flips that does indeed take my breath away.

She is breaking me down. So contagious. Making me ache all over.

My gut clenches, and I battle the throbbing in my jeans. She kneels on the chair, straddling Johnny's lap, and hovers over him, dominating him, inches from his face. Then she ties the gold ribbon around his neck and the other end to the chains still tightly bound around her breasts. I swallow hard, wanting to see those naked. She leans closer to him, dropping her head down so her hair engulfs his face, and I wonder what she smells like.

She lifts her arms like a swan, then drags her hair off his face as she arches away, slowly bending her back, reaching for her heels, and tightening the chains as she gets further away. Her hair hangs down off her head. I'm impressed with her flexibility, and that pose sends my mind dreaming of Kama Sutra positions we could enjoy together.

When she grabs the heels of her stilettos, the chains bust, letting the remnants of the corset melt down her hard abs, sliding into a pile of gold on Johnny's lap. I bite my tongue and hold my breath as a wave of lust racks my whole body.

He is one lucky birthday boy to have that gift unwrapped like that.

Then as she begins arching upright, my gut tightens into a hard knot. Her breasts are bare for all to see. Her nipples are painted with gold dust! The sight of them makes everything inside me burn hot. Plump, full, round, soft, and firm, they are begging for attention. When she pushes them together, a soft, desperate moan escapes my lips.

They are perfect!

Johnny leans his head down, trying desperately to sink his face between them. The thought of him touching her causes my jaw to clench, and that primal something that lives just under the surface dangerously wants me to jump up onto that stage, jerk her off him by her hair, smash my fist in his face, then drag her off somewhere to own, knowing this time once will not be enough.

She puts her fingertips on his forehead and pushes his face away. Then she stands up, spins around, and sits on his lap. Johnny lets out a frustrated roar and tries to get his arms loose.

Thank god, the son of a bitch is tied to that chair. If he touched her right now, I would crush him and enjoy it.

She stands, blows him a kiss, then dances straight to me. Her perfection fills my mind completely. Her golden orbs freely moving in rhythm with her stride. She stops at the edge of the stage, and my eyes devour her gorgeousness. Her features are Scandinavian. Her eyes are light, maybe blue, maybe green, maybe grey. Her lips are a dark soft pink, and a wave of passion washes over me.

I wonder what her sweet lips taste like.

She looks out at the darkness to connect with the crowd, yet she cannot see anyone. She smiles a beautiful smile, full of gentleness and hope. Her happiness radiates from her face, giving her a glow.

She turns away, and my eyes drop to devour her ass. It is as spectacular as the front. She grabs the stripper pole and flings her legs up, pushing herself upside down. She makes one complete revolution, then drops into a squat on her perfect ass. Holding onto the pole, she leans her torso away and bumps and grinds it. Everything in me wants her to do that to me.

Standing again, she struts away back to the birthday boy, and I watch her butt cheeks roll as she goes.

They are powerful glutes. Perfect for pounding!

When she arrives, she does the unthinkable. She takes her shoes off, then puts her foot between his legs and rubs him. I shift in my seat. Then she firmly grasps Johnny's chin in her hand, forces his face to hers, and leans down. Right before her lips touch his, she smiles, then turns his face away. She whispers in his ear, and he grins big, then she times her kiss on his cheek perfectly with the end of the song.

The spotlight goes off.

Silence and darkness again fall on the crowd. My senses are already tuned in and hyped up. Listening to hear her retreating footsteps, but I only hear the sounds of people shifting in the audience. No one is talking. Then I pick up on the sounds of footsteps approaching and see out of the corner of my eye the same two dancers in flamingo feathers untying Johnny and helping him back down to his table. His friends stand and pat him on the back or knuckle bump him when he arrives. He is all grins.

I know where his dreams will come from for a while. Hell, I know where mine will come from, from now on.

I drain my glass and place it on the table.

THUMP, THUMP, THUMP.

The song "Beautiful Drug" by the Zac Brown Band begins as four spotlights from the four corners of the room circle the crowd to the music. Like everyone else, I look around, searching for her. Then with the opening words about a death wish, the beams converge at the very top of the stripper pole.

"Wow," I say as the crowd collectively gasps.

Seary is positioned at the very top, doing a split in the air and rotating around it.

She has to be in incredible shape to have climbed that distance, and how in the hell did she get that red outfit and shoes on?

As the song plays about being high, being addicted, needing a hit of love, and not wanting to be saved, she spins, doing various splits. When the words say something about letting her hair down, she flips upside down and drops like a rock, then she clamps down on the pole, stopping with a hard jerk. The words mention hair standing up, and mine does. It's a daredevil move. She's fearless!

Unable to take my eyes off her like everyone in the room, we are glued to her. For the rest of the song, she owns the pole, and the way she moves on it drives me crazy with thoughts of hooking up with her.

She is so limber and strong. We could have so much fun!

When she gets to the landing, she lightly touches down, and I know the song is absolutely right. She is "a beautiful drug," and I'm at risk of being addicted to her.

When the song ends, another immediately begins. The runways have filled with dancers, and they are swaying to the music "Loved Me Back To Life."

Seary struts her stuff, dancing in and out of the girls down the runway, making her way to the stage. When she reaches it, right on cue, they all begin dancing a routine, but she is more expressive in hers. I'm enthralled with her moves and the fact that she makes the words resonate in my heart. Literally bringing it back to life. It's thumping hard for her.

When the words say strong hands and an open heart, I imagine my hands cupping her body, holding her tight against me, and cherishing her as I have never cherished anyone before, allowing her to see my pain. Then she spins across the stage and into the curtain, vanishing.

The applause is deafening. I whistle and stand, clapping as hard as anyone else while the other dancers run off the stage.

I turn back to see Bianca standing on the chair in front of Kip. She spins around to face him, wrapping her arms around his neck, pulling him tight into her chest as she looks down into his face. He gives me a blind thumbs-up, then puts his hands on her ass and squeezes her butt cheeks.

I walk by them, and Kip asks. "You good?"

"Yeah. Nature's calling."

"Hurry up. She's not finished, and I know you don't want to miss it."

I pat his back as I walk by. "Order me a double. Make it twin doubles. I'm gonna need it."

He laughs, and strangely Bianca doesn't say a thing, but I'm too distracted to give it much thought.

The floor is lit with soft red l.e.d. lights, and I find the men's room easily. It is full, and I wonder how many of them are here for the same reason. I enter the stall, lock it, lean my head back against the door, and breathe. I inhale and exhale deep breaths trying to gain control of my emotions. Images of Seary flash through my mind like a kaleidoscope of snapshots through the camera lens. I shake my head to clear it, but she won't go away. She's bouncing down the runway again toward me, and everything inside me wants to open my arms and wrap them around her. I try to push her out of my head, but I know that isn't going to happen, so I relieve myself, flush and open the stall door.

As I wash my hands, I look at myself in the mirror. My face appears calm and in control, but my eyes tell a different story. They look bewildered. I splash water on my face, then lean on the sink and stare again at my reflection.

The dude next to me asks, "Hey man, you alright?"

"Yeah. I'm cool. Just drank too much too fast."

I turn away and pull some paper towels off the machine to dry my hands. Then throw them in the garbage can on my way out, glancing back at my reflection before I face her again. The bewildered look is still there.

Dammit. I've screwed up coming here. I hang my head as I push the door open. She is going to be trouble.

When I step out the bathroom door, I lean up against the wall and wait, not ready to go close enough to face her again. The lights on the stage are illuminated, and my whole body tunes in to find Seary.

CHAPTER EIGHT

Siri

"Woo, y'all, we have a hyper crowd tonight." I tell James and the girls as I step into Beyoncé's "Dance For You" costume. He zips it up, then moves to snap the fishnet hose in the garter for me, while Beatrice stuffs my hair into a skull cap and secures my Beyoncé wig, as Tory applies the latex facial prosthetics and then quickly paints my face to look like the diva.

When they step back, James verifies my

transformation. Then he points to the concealed door that joins my dressing room and shoos everyone out.

Within minutes, the stage is set. The other dancers are in place, and he signals Cat. She opens the celebrity's dressing room door and tells me, "Queen Bee, we are ready for you."

I stand as Beyoncé and strut to the stage. Waiting for the curtain to rise and the music to start, I hear the crowd's noise. They are loud, which means they are happy, which makes me happy. I truly am living the dream.

When the people closest to the stage notice the curtain going up, a hush spreads across the auditorium. The sound of sirens in a raging thunderstorm silences the crowd completely. Beyoncé's heels click, and I sync my steps as I walk across the stage, slowly stripping off the raincoat. Then I turn my back to the crowd, take my position between the couch and the coffee table props placed on the stage and dance to the video.

Aurelius

I know Beyoncé is a big damn deal, but I could give a fuck less if she's in the house or not. Leaning against the wall, watching the dancer on stage, I wonder if she is Beyoncé or if she's the impersonator, Surreal.

A man leans against the wall beside me. I recognize the birthday boy and say, "Sup?" He gives me a head nod. "So, how torturous was it?"

He laughs and shakes his head. "Hell! Pure hell!"

I laugh with him, "Everyman's dream and worst nightmare."

He huffs. "That's for sure."

We watch the Beyoncé performance, lost in our own thoughts, then he adds, "I'll never forget her as long as I live."

I chuckle at that truth. "So what did she whisper in your ear?"

He grins, "She said in the cutest southern dialect, 'I'm going to give you a birthday peck on your cheek now, Sugar. Don't move! I'm warning you. If you turn your face to steal a kiss, I will turn Mr. Rooster down there into Miss Hen. Understand?"

We bust out laughing together.

"So she's not only sexy but sassy, too, huh?" I ask him.

"She's got some serious attitude."

"Sexy and sassy is a deadly combination."

"Yeah, it is." He stands, and I hold my hand out. "Happy Birthday, Brother."

He takes it and says, "Thanks." Then he walks back to his table. I watch him managing the maze, still not ready to return to mine.

Watching the remainder of the possible Surreal performance, I'm struck by the fact that if the dancer is indeed the impersonator, she is damn good!

By the time the curtain goes down, I'm back in charge of my raging beast and head back to the table. I'm halfway there when the curtain rises to reveal Surreal standing there. She has on the costume from the poster, and she looks hot as hell in it.

The crowd roars their approval. Surreal takes her bow, waves to the crowd, blows them kisses, then trots off.

A waitress walks by, and I reach out to stop her. "Tell me something, why is everyone so thrilled it was Surreal performing and not disappointed it wasn't Beyoncé?"

She laughs, "Simple. Surreal is our celebrity. She

is just as good as they are, but she's one of us. She's our star, and Vegas loves her."

"That makes sense."

When I arrive back at the table, Kip tells me the obvious. "Your drinks are here."

"Thanks." I sit down, take one and toss the whole thing back, pick the second one up and do it again, then slam the glass down. "Ah! That's better."

He whistles. "I don't know that I've ever seen you do that."

I give him a 'you're crazy' look. "What are you talking about? We've gotten wasted together plenty of times. Have you forgotten, or were you too wasted to remember?"

He chuckles. "Naw, man. That's not what I'm talking about."

Oh, that.

I look at this new quiet Bianca. She is staring at me, disengaged, which is entirely out of character for her. "What's in your craw?"

"Nothing."

That's girl code for 'something big,' but I lose focus when the THUMP and strobes bust the air again. My mind shouts 'no,' but the rest of me tunes in. I sit there struggling with myself and staring blankly at Bianca.

Could I walk out without a backward glance?

Siri

As soon as I step through the curtain, my team awaits me. James helps me strip out of my Surreal Black and Blue Baby. At the same time, Beatrice removes my wig and mask. Then she fluffs my hair with her supersonic gizmo and secures a headdress with white feathers. Tory slaps a gob of sticky goo between my legs and applies a mesh covering of little tiny white down feathers to cover any overexposure while I dance. When they step back, I hook my arms in the harness, and Cory flips the switch on the hydraulic lift, hurdling me through the air to the top of the ceiling, where he waits on a trapeze landing zone.

"Seary, you are on your game tonight." He compliments me as he helps me out of the harness and onto the platform.

I laugh and tease him, "Have you ever known me not to be?"

He chuckles, "No, I haven't. You always deliver a stellar performance."

I grab the rope, wrap it around my hand, and wait to jump and swing out over the crowd.

Aurelius

Immediately, the THUMP, THUMP, THUMP, and the matching strobes bust the air again.

"This Is What You Came For" by Calvin Harris, featuring Rihanna, begins to play.

Bianca nods and mouths, "She's on again."

I can't resist. I turn to look for Seary. A white flash of something flying through the air cuts the light's beam. Then the spotlight finds it and reveals Seary. She looks like an angel. Her white-blonde hair has large white feathers woven through it, and she is naked except for a patch of white feathers strategically placed over her slit and hiding her nipples. She performs an acrobatic dance using the rope, and hot desire for her pulses through me.

Knowing the lightning she is creating will shoot me in all the right places, I slump down in the chair and straighten my legs.

She lands gracefully on the runway, and a couple of oblivious men stand and wave cash at her, hoping she will come to the edge for the money. She skillfully maneuvers out of their reach. Then one drunk dude puts his hands on the stage and attempts to climb up.

The knot in my gut and my jaw seize simultaneously, but two men snatch him off instantly and take him down. Looking around now, I see men dressed in black, blending in with the audience, and I realize how tight her security is. Out of the corner of my eye, the drunken trespasser is subdued and quietly escorted out.

When she mounts the stripper pole in front of me once more, she proceeds to do things to it that I wouldn't have believed possible if I was not witnessing her undeniable talent.

Her gracefulness is a thing of beauty. Her timing is perfect. No movement is off. Her arms, legs, hands, and feet are pure poetry in motion as she moves up and down its length, dancing sensually.

She is a true artist.

When she drops to the bottom of the pole at the

song's end, she swings around it, taking a unique bow. The people around me rise, giving her a standing ovation, and I stand with them.

As she scans the crowd, waving, our eyes touch for barely an instant, but in that flash of time, her unadulterated beauty lodges itself firmly in my soul.

Shocked, I sit down with my eyes locked on Seary and acknowledge ... I want this sexy, sassy little stripper. I want her staring into my eyes, looking at me with the same look Easy has for her Badass Baby Daddy.

The music moves immediately into "Dangerous Woman" by Ariana Grande, and Seary backs up against the pole. Sliding down it, then right back up, she proceeds to seduce the room as she slinks her sexy, sassy self back to the stage, and like everything thing else she has done tonight, her dance and her song choice are spot on, speaking directly to my heart. When she vanishes from sight exactly on the song's last note, the crowd in the room explodes again with applause and cheers. I join in, bold and confident, knowing I always get what I want because I make it happen, and this will happen!

The announcer comes back on and thanks everyone on Seary's behalf. Knowing the show is over, the crowd collectively sits back down, and the noise level of intercommunication becomes loud. I look at Kip and Bianca as I turn my chair back around and scoot it up under our table. Kip is grinning from ear to ear at me, and I can't help the stupid grin that responds to his like a schoolboy who has just gotten caught stealing a kiss from his first crush.

Kip asks. "So... what did you think?"

"I think you were right. She's as hot as her name implies."

Bianca doesn't say a word, and she's not smiling. Her earlier answer 'nothing' returns to my mind, and I know I need to deal with the 'something big' that is 'nothing.' But the waitress returns and brushes my arm with her breasts as she leans in to pick up our empty glasses. "My name is Stacey. May I get you another round?"

"Yes, please. The same."

When she stands back up, her hip presses into my arm, and she smiles at me. "Excellent. I'll be more than happy to hook you up." The innuendo hangs in the air as she continues to hold my eyes and asks Kip and Bianca. "Would you two also like to reorder the same?"

I hear Kip say, "Yes."

"I'll be right back. Don't go anywhere." She tells me, then disappears again.

When I look over at Kip and Bianca, I expect to see her leaning on the table in her usual aggressive, jealous position, but instead, she is sitting in Kip's lap. Surprised, I ask her again. "What's in your craw?"

She gives me a look like it's a dumb question and repeats, "Nothing."

"Don't give me that bullshit, Bianca. Something is up with you."

Kip chuckles at us.

"Not with me. With you."

"What?" I frown at her.

She rolls her eyes. "It's nothing. I'm fine."

"Bianca, we've known each other for years. And in that time, you have never not challenged another woman who is in my presence. What's in your craw?" I stare at her.

"What's in my 'craw' Alabama boy isn't the question. What's in yours, or rather, who's in yours?"

I look at her, thinking about that and who she is implying.

Seary. Yeah, Seary is in my craw. First time I've ever had someone in there too.

For just a moment, I think about shrugging it off

and denying it, but then I realize no point. Bianca's right, and she knows she is right.

"Wait a minute. Wait just a damn minute! Are you telling me that you've just let it go, just like that?"

"No point anymore."

"What the hell?" I shake my head, confused by her certainty.

She laughs with confidence.

"Explain yourself," I demand.

She raises her eyebrows at me, and I know that was a turn-on for her.

"Listen, Aurelius. It's the way you looked at her."

I frown, knowing my tongue wasn't hanging out with drool dripping off it. I'm conscientious about my facial expressions. I raise my eyebrows at her and command more information.

She looks at Kip for help, and he says. "Don't look at me. I'm lost too."

She rolls her eyes like we are children.

Stacey comes back with our drinks and again brushes my arm with her breasts as she sets them down. I reach into my pants and pull out a tip for her. She grins as I stick it in her cleavage. "Thanks, Big Daddy."

Bianca says, "You're wasting your time, girlfriend. He's got Seary in mind."

She laughs and looks at her. "Then I'm not wasting my time at all. She doesn't do extracurricular activities." She looks down at me. "My shift ends in a couple of hours. We can hook up then if you're interested."

I smile at her and ask, "What if I'm gambling?"

"Then you'll need to go ahead and book a room. Let Beverly know you want me."

"Thanks." I smile at her, and she turns away, thinking I'm going to. I look back at Bianca. "Okay. You're correct. I do have Seary in mind. Why aren't you upset by that?"

She laughs. "The battle is lost. No need to fight for it."

I frown at her, unsure which direction to pursue with her implications. "Are you telling me if I had brought a date around you, you would have backed off?"

"No."

I frown harder.

"What I'm telling you is the look on your face when you watched Seary is the same look on Kip's face when he looks at me."

"And what look is that?"

She smiles at me and turns to look at Kip. She kisses his lips, pulls back, and runs her fingers down his temple across his jawline. He looks at her, mesmerized. She looks around at me and states, "It's a complete commitment."

"Commitment?"

Her soft look says she's right, and I'll discover it on my own.

"What makes you so sure?"

"I've known you a long time and pressured you the entire time. You have never given in, not because you aren't attracted to me and not because you wouldn't dig it, but because you respect our commitment too much. I got that, but I knew I could convince you eventually. This? Her? What I see in your eyes? What I see on your face? That? I will never overcome."

I don't answer. I don't have an answer. I don't know anything right now except I need to drink. I reach for one of my doubles and slam it down. She and Kip take theirs, and Bianca raises hers to me and then throws it back. I look at the stage and watch without seeing the dancer on the pole.

The three of us sit silently for a bit longer, then I throw my last shot back and tell them. "I'm going to go gamble. I've seen enough for one night."

Kip pushes Bianca off his lap and stands with

me. I shake his hand, and he says. "I hope Lady Luck smiles down on you."

"Yeah. Thanks."

"How long are you staying?"

"I'm flying home Wednesday."

"Ok. Let me know if you need anything else."

"Will do." I look at Bianca. She is smiling up at me. Leaning down, I kiss the top of her head, "Laters, Tough girl." Then I walk away.

As I exit the gentleman's club portion of Been Jammin', it's like I'm leaving behind the best thing that's happened to me, unresolved, and it's a haunting feeling. Bianca's words weigh heavy on my mind, knowing in my heart she is right. Seary got under my skin, pierced it, scarring it forever.

Beverly sits at a table alone on the fake patio area —no time like the present to seize an opportunity to move forward. I walk over.

She has an iPad and a drink. She looks up when I pull a chair out and ask, "May I?"

"Certainly," she smiles. "Did you enjoy Seary's show?"

"I did. That's what I want to talk to you about."

She sits back in her chair. "May I get you a drink?"

"No. I'm good. Thank you."

"What can I do for you then?"

"I want to book a private session in a VIP room."

"Excellent." She sits back up.

"I'm counting on you to make my fantasy come true."

Laughing, she pulls her iPad to her. "I can help you with that."

"There will be a big bonus for you if you do."

"I like big bonuses. Who's the lucky girl?"

I pause for emphasis, making her stop and focus on my choice. Remembering what Stacey said about Seary not doing extracurricular activities and wanting Beverly to know I'm serious —committed. I wait until our eyes connect, then I deepen my voice and answer. "Seary."

She looks surprised and says impulsively, "She isn't available."

I smile with confidence. "You didn't check."

"I don't have to." She shakes her head. "I already know. She isn't available."

I look away, then look back, letting my eyes speak to my intentions. I am determined. No is not the correct answer. "Ask whoever you need to ask, but ask. I intend to make this happen."

Her look is just as determined as mine, but her

confidence is not similar. "I'll ask, but don't get your hopes up."

"Come on.... You make it sound like she doesn't do them because she's the star. But we both know she will for enough money."

"I didn't say she doesn't do them. I said she was unavailable."

"Ask anyway and get back to me." I stand, push my chair back in, then turn and walk away.

Seary's body dances in my mind. Gambling is out of the question. I couldn't focus even if I wanted to right now. Passing the Steakhouse, the smell draws me in. I'm hungry and need to eat before I get on the highway.

The hostess asks, "How many?"

"One."

Damn. That sounded lonely.

She sits me at a table for two, facing a couple having a romantic dinner together. I try not to watch them, but it's impossible. With each romantic kiss, they exchange or intimate laughter they share, loneliness surrounds me.

While the waiter takes my order, the couple leaves. Sitting there staring at nothing, my mind defaults back to Seary.

She is going to be a force to be reckoned with.

CHAPTER NINE

My Porterhouse steak is cooked to perfection, and I concentrate on enjoying every delicious mouthful. After checking out, I walk through the casino. Rebecca's table is full, and people are standing around watching. Then cheers erupt from the enthusiastic crowd. I'm not in the mood for all that. I'll pass.

Once outside the casino, I hand the valet my ticket. When he returns with my corvette, I hold out a $20. "Where's the service entrance?"

He looks down at the tip and says. "I'm new. I don't know." He smiles, reaching for the tip.

I pull it back and add another $20 to it. "Which side of the building do the employees enter for work?"

He grins and says, "Northside."

"Very good. Thank you." I take my key and give him the tip.

"You're welcome. Thank you."

When I leave the parking lot, I hook a left and drive around to scope out the entrance on the north side of the club. It's the parking garage.

Without knowing what she drives and if they have designated spots, that's a bust. No way will I be able to catch her going in or out. Too random.

I head out onto the highway and turn toward my house. My thoughts swirl around Seary. Where is she from? Where did she study dance? I thought I was immune to lust, but she busted that myth down and stomped on it. Is Bianca right? Commitment? Wow, what a word choice. Commitment. I guess my focus on her was utterly committed. I certainly wasn't aware of anyone else in the room. And I am definitely going to commit to having her withering under me, moaning my name.

I arrive, still lost in my thoughts, park, then head upstairs to take a quick shower and wash off the cigarette smoke before bed. Stripping, I toss my clothes in the dumbwaiter and push the button to send them to the laundry room. I turn the water on and hope the cold water will chill my lust-filled mind, and I can get in and out quickly. I'm beat. Stepping directly under the waterfall, I gasp when the cold liquid hits my head, runs down my chest, and between my legs.

Brrr! That's painful! Shivering, I force myself to wait for the warm water to arrive. Leaning into it, I wash away the suds, being careful not to stimulate my dick. When I step out, I grab a towel, dry off, then walk naked to the bed and collapse on it. I'm asleep before I can crawl under the covers.

My eyes pop open. Johnny said, 'in the cutest southern accent.'

"She's a southern girl." I smile and fall back to sleep.

A sexy siren, wrapped in gold threads, sings and dances, calling to me.

I'm hypnotized and walk like a zombie to her. Taking the gold thread she offers, I pull it hard, and she spins like a top. Her hair fans out, and the speed of her spinning creates a blurry image, showing off her voluptuous hourglass shape.

Big breasts and ass, tiny waist. I moan.

The thread unwinds and falls silent on the ground.

I stand watching, waiting, hungry to see her gold

tips as her spinning body slows down. Desperate to bury my face and get lost in them.

Suddenly, she stops and stands naked before me. Her breasts rebound and bounce against each other.

I reach out to cup them.

She places the end of the gold thread in my hand, and my fingers wrap around it. She pulls it. I try to take a step, but something is blocking my feet.

I look down.

The gold thread is wrapping around my legs and turning into a heavy gold rope.

When I look back at the sexy siren, she has turned into a blonde Wonder Woman.

Her face is fierce. Brave. Strong.

We stand there staring at each other. Supremely confident. Equal.

She smiles, and warmth floods my body. Telepathically, with a sensual southern drawl, she asks my heart, "What do you feel?"

I look down at my chest, compelled to answer her. Words float from my chest, intertwining with each other —Lust —Love.

She reaches her hand out, and the word Lust rushes into it, and Love returns to hover in front of me.

Her smile fades, "You are no different from the others." Slowly, she backs away, fading into the dark.

"NO!" I cry out and sit up in bed. I look around, disoriented, searching for her. The coldness of the dark makes me shiver, and I lay back, sinking in the loneliness.

Staring at the ceiling, the dream still holding my mind captive, the horror of loneliness threatens to swallow me. My PTSD button is being pushed.

Breathe! Breathe!

I put my feet on the floor, stand up and move to open the blinds. It's still dark. I pace, but it doesn't help. I need to run.

Going into the closet, I throw on a pair of compression briefs, sweatpants, a hoodie, and sneakers. I run down the stairs, through the front door, and out the gate without thinking of anything but extracting the feeling and clearing it out.

I run to the end of the drive, hook a right and run to the entrance of the golf course. I run hole after hole until the sun has risen, and I'm not alone anymore.

Clothes drenched with sweat, I walk back up to my house. Entering, I hear the sounds of humming coming from the interior.

Maria!

I smile. Tiptoeing, I walk through the house until I'm standing outside the laundry room and waiting with my back flat against the wall to scare her when she exits. She turns on the dryer, humming, and then she heads for the door. I hold my breath and prepare to pounce.

As soon as she exits, I grab her and yell.

She screams, and her knees buckle. I hug her up tight to me, laughing my ass off.

"HOLY JESUS!" She laughs, slipping her arms around my waist, burying her face in my chest, and we share a good laugh together. "You are such an asshole!"

As soon as the humor fades, I release her, and she sticks her tongue out. Then disses me with, "You stink. Go get cleaned up while I go grocery shopping. I will use you as a guinea pig for a new recipe." She flips me off as she leaves out the side door.

Laughing, I strip, leaving my stinky clothes in the laundry room. Then head upstairs for another quick shower. While I wait for Maria to return, I go into my construction office to review the renovation I've planned for the east wing.

When Maria returns, I help her bring the food inside. Then I spend the remainder of the day eating and being her guinea pig for several new dishes, laughing and cutting up with her, teasing her that this taste terrible as I eat every mouthful, and helping her film and edit her clips. We finish washing the dishes together, grab a bottle of wine and go out on the patio to watch the sunset.

Sitting with my friend, Maria starts to talk, "You know, Aurelius. Every time I see the sunset from here, the burnt orange glow changing into deep scarlet red on the rock, I think of how passion would look if it had colors. Like a fire that flames orange, then, as it gets hotter, burns red until it's so hot, it will scorch your heart no matter that you've made it as hard as that rock. You know?" She looks at me. "I miss that. I miss the passion of love." She stands and says, "Goodnight." Then walks back inside without a backward glance.

I'm left alone, watching the vibrant sunset and seeing a flame named Seary dance in front of my eyes, and I feel the place in my heart she has already scorched. It's warm and feels strangely free.

I wait until the sunlight is completely gone, then I go back into the house, put my wine glass in the sink next to Maria's, and head upstairs to change. I have to see her dance again. Crazy as it is, I have to know if the lust she sparked last night was a fluke or if it was real.

. . .

Driving my Jaguar tonight, I get in the long line for valet parking. Waiting patiently, thinking about the construction in the East Wing and whether or not I'll go to Italy this year with the family for Christmas or decide to come out here to work on it instead, a limousine pulls past.

I wonder who is in it? The car door opens, and I see a pair of stilettos appear. My heart skips a beat. But then I see a redhead exit, and my heart returns to beating normally. I pull up under the canopy, and an epiphany hits me between the eyes.

What if she is driven to work and uses the front door? It wouldn't be the first time a club asked their stars to promote their show by allowing the fans close access.

When the valet takes my information and keys, I ask, "Is the redhead a star?"

"Only to us. She's part owner, but we do have celebrities quite frequently for our high-stakes backroom poker games. You never know who will show up. I've opened limo doors for Dana White, Joe Rogan, and Toby Keith."

I pull $20 out of my pocket. "Does Seary arrive in a limo?"

"Ah...." He grins at me and winks as he takes the money. "She does, but you're early. She doesn't arrive until roughly two hours before her show." He pulls the tip from my fingers, "Good luck."

I walk into the casino and walk straight back to Been Jammin'. When I arrive at the hostess podium, she politely asks, "Do you have a reservation?"

"Negative. I want a reservation," I state and smile.

"Which bar?"

"The Gentlemen's Club."

"There isn't anything available tonight, but I can put you down for tomorrow night."

I look away, trying not to show my displeasure at having to wait another night. I'm not the kind of man that waits for things to work out. I'm a take charge and make things work out kind of man. "Yes. Please. Put me down for tomorrow night." I give her my name and contact information, then walk away a few feet. Stop, slowly turn around as I reach into my pocket, and thumb through a wad of cash. Walking back up, I flash a $50, lean in, and whisper to her, "I forgot your tip. Excuse me."

Her head tilts, and she smiles at the bill. "That's very considerate of you."

"If a table becomes available, please give me a call. I want to fill it."

She smiles as she pulls the money from my fingers, "I'll add you to the waiting list."

I flip out another $50 and hold it up for her to accept. "This is yours if you move me to the top of the list."

She takes it and says, "You'll be my first call."

I verify I'm listed in the number one slot.

She laughs, "Mr. Moore, if there is a third bill, I will guarantee we will have a cancelation tonight."

"Deal," I peel off another. "If I can sit in one of the elevated booths in the center before Seary's show starts, there are two more for you."

"Deal."

As I add the extra bills to her tip, she says, "Be here at midnight."

"I'll see you then," I wink at her and watch as she removes someone named Merle Hollis and writes Aurelius Moore on the chart.

Walking away, I feel like a gambler feeding an addiction.

Heading back to the entrance, I check the time. Seary should be arriving shortly. Sitting at a slot machine close enough to see outside, I watch the vehicles coming, absentmindedly feeding it $20's and pushing the buttons, letting the reel spin pissing money into it. At around 9:55, five big men in suits arrive and stand by just inside the lobby. "Humph, bodyguards."

At 10:00 sharp, a limo pulls up. The security detail walks out, and four turn their backs on the limo. Effectively signaling that no one is allowed to approach the star. The fifth walks to the limo and opens the door.

Red Converse tennis shoes and distressed skinny jeans appear first, followed by a ball cap pulled down snugly, shielding her face. Then she stands and exits the vehicle.

It's Seary.

She's wearing a red cable ribbed sweater that accentuates her plump breasts. Propped up on top of them is one thick braided blonde ponytail. Instantly my heart revs up to three thousand RPMs. The elegant way she moves blocks the breath in my throat. The men casually surround her, creating a loosely bound human shield to escort her inside.

She smiles up at the lead man and speaks to him. Their conversation reflects friendship. He's been with her a long time.

Impulsively, I hit the cash-out button to intercept her path. No plan in mind. Shooting from the hip. I'll come up with something.

Bells start clanging, and the light on top of my machine starts spinning. I freeze. What the hell? I hit the jackpot? Dammit. Casino etiquette requires jackpot winners to wait for the cashier to come.

I turn back to watch Seary and her entourage heading my way. She peers through them to look at my machine. Smiling, happy someone has won.

My breath hitches, and my heart skips a beat. She's not wearing a speck of makeup, and she's absolutely stunning without it. Her beauty is real. Not created.

Her eyes shift to locate the winner, and I brace myself to meet them. Passing within a few feet of me, my gut draws up, needing to feel something genuine when our eyes connect. But right before the direct connection, the bodyguard's stride blocks us, and my eyes trail after her retreating figure. Her ass looks perfect in those jeans.

I turn to the lady sitting two machines down and tell her. "Congratulations, ma'am. You just won the jackpot. It's all yours."

She looks startled by my words, then recovers

quickly. "Thank you! What a nice young man you are!"

As I walk away, I hear her friend add. "What a handsome young man too!"

I close the distance behind Seary, analyzing how her detail proceeds and how they assess the crowd. They are trained bodyguards on the lookout for prowlers and possible stalkers. An older couple waves at Seary, calling her by name, and she waves back, then stops to chitchat and pose for a picture. She slides between them, and they hug her uptight while one of her goons takes the picture.

I circle to get a better view but stay far enough away not to be seen. It's hard to tell if her goons are more for crowd control than safety, but the way their suits are cut, they could be packing weapons.

They continue without incident, and I fall in line behind them to the fake patio at the Club entrance and watch as she disappears from my view.

Knowing she's here getting ready to perform sets me on edge, and I decide to wait at the bar. Wedging myself between the men crowded around a nearly topless bartender, I order a Crown and coke tonight. UFC is on the screen overhead, and I absentmindedly watch the two dudes grappling on the ground for a position, letting my mind go over the details and formulate a plan of action. I haven't played this game before. Hmm. Do I begin my seduction first? Her team is punctual, which means predictable. I could work that to my advantage. Do I get in her path and get noticed? Getting her alone in a VIP room is a must and the ideal scenario, but if all else fails, I can book a customized sexual fantasy.

I decide to text Darren while I wait.

I'm at the Club. Bart runs a top-notch establishment.

A couple of minutes go by unanswered. He's probably asleep.

And Seary?

I saw her dance last night. Pure magic.

Awesome news!

My recommendation is to invest.

Excellent! I'll let Bart know I'm a go. Do you want in too?

No. Conflict of interest.

Thanks for your help, Buddy.

No problem.

Someone touches my shoulder. I look to see who is sliding up next to me.

"Mr. Moore." Beverly smiles like a cat who just got a bowl full of milk. "Do you need my help getting a table tonight?"

"No. I have a reservation."

She nods. "I've just left Seary's dressing room."

"And?"

"Trust me on this. You won't want to miss a single second of tonight's entertainment." She pats my back.

"And?" I raise my eyebrows for an answer to the real question.

"Look me up afterward. I'll be sitting right over there again tonight when you leave. I have news."

"Perfect."

"Enjoy the show."

"I'm sure I will."

I turn my attention back to the MMA fighters bloodying each other up overhead, but I don't see them. She has good news. Otherwise, she wouldn't have spoken.

My alarm goes off at 11:55pm, and I walk back to the podium with $200 in my hand. The same hostess greets me and says, "Right this way, Mr. Moore. Tara, I'm going to seat him myself. Cover for me."

Tara checks me out and grins. "Sure."

I follow her to an elevated booth just outside the first row of tables. Designed to seat ten people, the view of the stage is perfect, and I give her the tip when she sits me. The room is packed again, and the dancers on the stage are excellent, high-quality talent.

"THUMP, THUMP. THUMP, THUMP" The strobes blind me. My abs harden as I get ready to see Seary in action. The correlation between the beating bass and my increased heart rate gives me an instant erection in anticipation of seeing her nearly naked body just a few feet away, as well as the strobing lights and the throbbing it's now doing isn't lost on me. Sexually suggestive. Brilliantly played!

Tonight, Seary doesn't start with an opening act. She dances out onto the stage alone without music. She doesn't have on a stitch of clothes. Her entire body, including her hair, is painted deep red and dark purple. It's powerful and profound.

When the music does start, it's "Wild" by Troye Sivan featuring Alessia Cara. The words seep into my soul as I watch her mesmerizing dance. Careful not to expose herself, she bends, twirls, splits, and dances wildly. I'm guilty, like the lyrics say, of trying not to fall and keeping the old protective walls around my heart. But it's hopeless.

I can't turn away. This woman drives me absolutely wild! Dammit! I want her so bad. I've got to have her!

When the song ends, she stops dancing and stands motionless on the stage. The room falls silent. A group of four mimes, Jabbawockeez, run onto the stage and begin looking at her. They step closer, examining her with their eyes and mimes. Then they huddle up, talk, look at her, then huddle, then look at her, nod their heads, high-five, and break. Two run off, and two walk over, take her arms, raise them to shoulder height, and then push them over her head. The other two reappear, bringing a long pole, paint bucket, and brush. They mime discussing who will get to do what, and they flip a coin. The two losers pick up the pole, hoist it over their heads, place Seary between them, dip down so her hands can latch on, and lift her off her feet. She hangs suspended. The other two take the paint bucket and brush, arguing over who gets to paint her. In my mind, little increments of time begin to tick off as I realize only her strong grip holds her entire body weight. When the two arguing finally get down to dipping the brush in the paint, my heart seizes when it comes out of the bucket.

It's the same gold paint she wore last night!

The memory of those taut tips dangling right before me sends my hand to grab my hard-on to stifle the starting throbbing. The song "Can't Stop The Feeling!" by Justin Timberlake begins to play, and the paintbrush is held out toward her body. The mimes, holding the pole, dance around so the brush applies paint. They stop when it thins so it can be dipped again in the bucket, and the painters swap. Each time they stop and become distracted, dipping the paint in the bucket, Seary's body begins to dance, hanging from the pole. When they return to her to apply the paint, she freezes, holding awkward poses, demonstrating her incredible strength.

The whole routine is funny, seductive, and powerful. When the song ends, the painters clap their hands and admire their work. She has a gold stripe the width of the painter's brush that wraps her body—starting at her hairline and winding down around those plump breasts, around her toned abs, around her butt, and down one of her muscular legs. The THUMP, THUMP, THUMP, and strobes begin again, and those two run off the stage, but the other two continue holding the pole.

The next song starts, and it's "Scream" by Usher. Seary swings her body for momentum and flips herself upside down onto the top of the pole. She slowly lowers her feet to it, then springs off, flipping and landing like a cat. The two men look shocked and flee from her. The lights on the stage go dark, and the body paint glows. She begins to dance like nothing I've ever seen before. It's like liquid glowing. My entire body clenches. She mimics withering, and it looks like rippling water. My mind locks up. Then she's dancing, moving her hips mimicking lovemaking, which looks like waves. Knowing I could do that to her all night until we both scream makes me even more determined to possess her and share my skills.

We will be good together!

Immediately she transitions into "Pillowtalk" by Zayn. I feel her dance interpretation deep inside me.

Sex is a paradise and a war zone.

The show's last song is "Hollow" by Tori Kelly, and it expresses how fragile she is—wanting to be wrapped and filled like a cup because her vessel is hollow. But she longs to be understood.

My heart hurts for her and, therefore, for me, needing to hold her close, cherish her, and protect her.

She ends the dance standing in the exact same spot in the exact same silent pose. The mimes return with a big barrel and stand behind her. They swing it, then heave it over her head and dump all the water in it on her. The paint washes away, and she is left naked, soaking wet, bare, bronzed flesh for everyone to see.

Stunning! She is the most beautiful creature I have ever laid eyes on.

Then they lower the barrel down over her, topple it, and pick it up, carrying her off. Right at the curtain, she sticks her head out and blows kisses to the crowd. The whole place sounds like a bomb went off as they erupt with cheers.

I leave without looking back to find Beverly, knowing I'll do whatever it takes to make this woman mine, and she will be mine over and over and over again.

CHAPTER
TEN

"Mr. Moore." Beverly's smile is confident. "Did you enjoy tonight's show?" She pushes her iPad away from her.

"Yes, I did. That body paint was hot."

She laughs. "I thought you would enjoy that. She was being painted when I walked in."

"So, tell me, have they agreed? I'm anxious to meet her."

"No doubt. They want me to discuss a few things with you first."

I hear Stacey's voice from last night say, 'She doesn't do extracurricular activities.' I brace for impact.

"Seary is our headlining star and tied directly to our brand."

"I understand that."

"Then you understand that she is an extremely valuable asset."

"I do."

"She's someone we must protect as well."

"And? Your point?"

"If you agree to all the terms, you must also pass a security background check."

I smirk, "Ok. I agree."

"You'll need to provide at least five personal references as well. We will be discrete and not reveal why we are inquiring."

"I'm ok with that too." I reach into my pants pocket to get a business card. I lay it on the table and slide it to her. "This is my Chief Operating Officer. She'll be instructed to give you the information you request."

She takes the card and tucks it inside the flap of her iPad. "Seary's time is minimal and therefore very valuable. Being our headliner isn't her only obligation."

"Name her price."

"Before we go there, we want you to understand what a valuable commodity she is. She is one of a kind."

"Oh, trust me when I say I fully understand that

she is one of a kind." I smile at her, hoping to assure her. She smiles back, but her eyes show she doesn't seem to get my level of commitment, so I add before she continues her 'justification for this price' sales pitch. "I'll pay $100,000 for a private VIP room to be alone with Seary for a two-hour exclusive session."

Her eyes nearly pop out of her face, and she clears her throat. "Excuse me?"

"I'll pay $100,000 ... for a private VIP room ... to be alone with Seary... for a two-hour ... exclusive session."

Her jaw sags as she looks incredulously at me.

I smirk and add. "Plus, if she agrees after our first meeting, I want an additional 2 hours every two weeks."

She blinks rapidly at me, clearly not expecting this, trying to decide what course of action she needs to take. "I'll put forth your offer and get back to you."

"I'd prefer you to put forth my offer now."

She studies my face and sees my determined look. "Yes. Ok." She pulls her iPad to her. I watch patiently while she gets her shit together and opens a chat with someone. I shift in my seat to read the texts upside down.

She types.

Are you available to chat?

YES. WHAT'S UP?

I'M WITH MR. MOORE DISCUSSING SEARY.

AH. STANDBY. I'M IN THE DRESSING ROOM.

Beverly smiles at me. "Just a moment."

OK. Is there a question about the vetting requirements?

NO. HE IS A GO.

EXCELLENT. THE PRICE IS FIRM. WE WON'T TAKE LESS. I THOUGHT I MADE THAT CLEAR.

Her satisfied cat smile returns.

You did, but he has made an offer with other conditions I'm not comfortable approving. I need your ok.

WHAT IS HIS OFFER?

HE WANTS TWO HOURS ALONE WITH HER. AN EXCLUSIVE SESSION.

TWO HOURS?

THAT'S CORRECT!

I DON'T KNOW ABOUT THAT.

HE'S OFFERING $100K.

$100,000 FOR 2 HRS?

THAT'S CORRECT.

STANDBY.

She smiles again at me. "They are discussing it."

"I can read it," I tell her, and her smile broadens.

"I believe you've shocked them too."

I smile. "Perhaps you should go ahead and tell them I want to be on a two-week rotation too." She grins, and I realize she must be paid on some commission structure.

She types.

Plus, he wants an additional two hours every two weeks.

YOU'RE JOKING, RIGHT?

NO, SIR! NOT JOKING.

YOU'RE IMPRESSION? IS HE A CRAZY ECCENTRIC?

She smiles and looks at me from under her lashes.

> He seems normal enough. Didn't bat an eye at the background checks.

> Ask him.

I laugh at that. "Tell him or them, or her, that I'm neither crazy nor eccentric, just very successful at a very young age, very rich, very private, and very picky."

She types that in verbatim.

> Damn. Ok then. I wasn't expecting this. Shifting things around. Standby.

We smile at each other, knowing they will make this happen. The thought of two hours in a room with Seary alone makes my cock very happy, and while I stare at the iPad waiting for the date. My mind begins to plan how to fill the room with roses and magnolias for our first session. The scent of natural beauty will fill it. I'll tie it together with a compliment on her natural beauty, and my seduction into her mind will begin. As the time ticks off, my eyes drift to stare blankly out at the people surrounding us. I'll wear a tuxedo. All black. No boxer briefs, so my cock can be seen without being exposed. I'll have champagne and dinner catered. I'll focus the entire time on discovering who she was, who she is, and what makes her tick. No sex, but I will nail her with a kiss at the end of the night that promises fireworks the next time.

The iPad lights back up and draws my eyes. Beverly looks down and says. "Well, this is romantic, Mr. Moore. The first available is Valentine's Day."

I can't control my outburst. "Are you fucking kidding me?"

Her eyes are startled by my outburst.

"No, sir. That's what the date is." She spins her iPad around so I can read it myself.

"That's three months from now!" My shock heightens my tone.

"Yes, sir. It is." She apologizes. "That must be the first available date. She is swamped, and the Holiday season is coming up. I know many girls take vacations during January too. I'm not sure about Seary, but perhaps that's why." She offers to calm me.

"Ask if a shorter time is available sooner." I point to the iPad. As she spins it back around to ask, I add. "Same price." That should work. Perhaps they are only negotiating now. I lean my arms on the table, anxious for the answer. My heart is holding my body hostage.

> Offer my apologies, but that's the first available day she doesn't have anything booked. She's a workaholic.

I stand up, and my chair almost tips over. I command her to "Book it!"

Walking through the casino, heading outside to get some fresh air, I see only the floor directly in my path, hear nothing but my blood pounding in my ears, and my thoughts circling inside my mind.

Seary. Three months. Dammit! How am I going to make it three months? The thought of returning to Italy to my studio to satisfy my sexual needs passes through it, but only for a fleeting moment. I know I won't be back there until after I've indulged myself with Seary, and that might be a while. If ever again. Seary has changed everything for me. Incredible as that sounds, I hear the truth in my heart and soul.

I exit the door and keep going past the valet station down the drive. I hook a left and walk. My pace is fast and determined. Weaving in and out of the flow of people, I head nowhere in particular. My mind is tormenting me with the images of her red, purple, and golden glow. The way she looks. The way she moves. Her body. Her dance. Three damn months. I have to wait three fucking months! I've finally found the one woman who has set my heart on fire and lit a flame burning inside me as I have never experienced before. Awakening feelings that I feared I was incapable of feeling.

I laugh aloud at the irony of the whole thing. Right when I acknowledge she could be the one, she's pushed out of my grasp. But I will wait with the patience of a hunter.

"LEAVE ME THE HELL ALONE! OR I'M GONNA MESS YOU UP!"

I stop and look around. I've walked five blocks North without realizing it. The building I just passed is an abandoned warehouse I purchased a year ago but haven't renovated yet. In the low light, I can make out two men squared off between the building and the adjacent vacant lot. There looks to be a makeshift tent to the right under some trees.

"Old man, you ain't gonna do nothin' but give me what I want, or I'm going to take it from you."

"What do you want?" I ask as I head in.

Three dudes dressed in dark clothes wearing hoodies pulled up over their heads lean against the building. As I get closer, alert to my approach, they push off and stand up. They are big but young punks.

"Mind your own damn business." The old man says without looking at me.

"Yeah. Mind your own damn business." The younger man agrees.

"I am minding my own damn business. I own the damn property you're standing on."

That revelation makes them all stop arguing and turn toward me. "What do you want from the old man?"

"They want my Special Forces Ranger knife." He smiles at them, "But I ain't part'n with it."

"How about you give it to me?"

"Why the fuck would I do that?"

"'cause they can't take it off me."

"They can't take it off me either."

I walk closer. Going slow to keep everyone calm. I'm guessing this is a gang initiation. The young men eye me, and I stare them down. They are confident that four on one or four on two are odds they can win.

"Give me the knife, old man. I got your back." I hold my hand out for the knife, and all hell breaks loose. The old man turns it on me and lunges. I sidestep him, grab his forearm, twist it behind his back, and take it from his fingers. Then I shove him to the ground, step over him, and confront his assailants.

With a deranged grin, tossing it nimbly from hand to hand, I dare them to be brave. It is equally balanced like my buck knife. "You think accosting an old man makes you a gangsta? It only makes you a coward. Do you think four-on-one is good enough odds? Bring it on."

I sniff the air and growl. "Ah! I've missed the smell of sweat, fear, panic, and *fresh blood*." They all stop as one, realizing I'm dead serious about that. Punks!

I flip the knife end over end, grasp the blade, bring it by my ear, cock my arm, flip my wrist, step to my target, and fling the knife with all my force. The loud thud it makes when it hits and the vibrating sound it makes as it settles down inside its new home draws every eye to the tree —all but mine.

As soon as I release the knife, I close the distance on the ringleader and smash my fist in his face. Before he can fall to the ground, I hit him two more times. He's out cold when he lands, and it's the second loud thud the punks hear. They turn their eyes big as moons on me, and I smash my fist in the face of the next closest one. He wobbles but doesn't go down. I shove him out of the way while I step over the unconscious body and draw my fist back to attack bully number three. He steps back, turns, and runs after bully number four.

"You better run, you worthless piece of shit!" I yell after them, then look down when something grazes my leg. Bully number two is dragging the leader out from under me. I stare him down, and he says. "Yeah. I learned my lesson. Don't fuck with old folks."

"I saved someone's life tonight. It might have been yours." I tell him, "Old soldiers don't go down without a fight. Some of us even enjoy them, but others play to win no matter the cost."

He looks past me at the old man walking to where his knife is in the tree. Then he squats down, puts his buddy on his shoulder, then carries him to the street. I hear the rumble of a car coming down the road and hope this doesn't turn into a drive-by shooting as I walk to the old man.

"You a Seal or something?" He asks me.

"Nope. Just an Army Aviator."

He laughs, "Damn, Flyboy! Thought you were a real soldier."

I laugh with him, "Marine?"

"Oorah!"

He holds his hand out, and I shake it. "Thanks."

"You're welcome. It looks good there. You should leave it."

"Yeah, I think it's safe there."

"You got food tonight?"

"I ate at the shelter."

"Alright. I hear they are good people."

"Yeah." He pats me on the back. "Thanks again."

"Sure." I turn around and head back. My mind is clear, and the tension, along with the frustration, is gone.

As I walk, I start making my plans. I may not be able to taste Seary's sweet southern sexiness for three more months, but that won't stop me from preparing for a long-term arrangement with her. I've got changes to make to the East Wing of my house.

CHAPTER
ELEVEN

FEBRUARY 14

THE JET TOUCHES DOWN, and.I stretch, smiling. I text Maria.

Just touched down. Be there after I visit the Club.

HAVE A GOOD TIME. WE'RE HAVING BLACK BARBECUE PORK CHOPS. DON'T BE LATE.

YUM!

Leaving the airport, I drive straight to Been Jammin'. When I arrive, Jimmy recognizes my Jag and positions himself to park it for me. When it's my turn, he opens my door. "My man, Moore. You're here early."

I step out. "I'm here to ensure everything is ready for tonight."

"Tonight? You mean tonight's the night?"

I chuckle as I hand him my keys. "Yes, it is."

"Are you finally going to tell me who?"

"Nope." My smile feels like it's brighter than the sun.

Walking through the casino, I head for Rebecca's table. She smiles a warm greeting when she sees me approaching. "Aurelius, are you nervous?"

I sit down at her table. "Nervous? No. Excited." I give her my Been Jammin' card, and she swipes it, then slides it back with a stack of chips. I gamble at her table while we visit. "Has everything been delivered?"

"Last time I checked, everything was here, and the crew was setting it up." She grins. "I don't know anyone who deserves each other more than you two. You're both fucking awesome, and I hope, no, I know you two will hit it off together."

"You haven't told anyone?"

"Nope. I've kept your secret. I asked around, and no one knows who will be entertained in the room tonight." She laughs. "No one suspects it's Seary, so she hasn't told anyone either."

"Thanks. This should be epic."

"I can't wait to tell her I've kept your secret all these months and helped you plan it."

"I appreciate your help in making this come together."

"No problem. I'm glad I could. Are you going in to see the room before time?"

"No. I think I'll wait too. So, how's your love life? Any special plans for tonight?"

She smiles. "Monty says he's got a surprise for me. I told him this morning that just waking up beside him was the best Valentine's Day gift I could have received, but he says he has something special for me. Not to work late."

"Any idea what it could be?"

"No, and I love surprises, so I didn't snoop around before coming to work either."

"Have you gotten him anything?"

"I saw this sexy teddy yesterday window shopping. I'm going to stop by on my way home and pick it up."

"He'll like that." I grin at her.

I play several more hands of Blackjack with her, but I can't concentrate. The man sitting next to me says. "Dude. You seriously should consider a new dealer. You're losing your ass here."

"That's a clue to get out of here," I tell them, then slide my chips back. "That's your tip, Rebecca."

"Aurelius. I'm speechless." She tells me with tears in her eyes.

I stand up, give her a wink, and tell her. "A small token of thanks. Happy Valentine's Day."

"Oh my gosh. You're the best!"

Driving to the house, I reflect on all the different shows I've watched Seary perform over these three months. My favorites so far were the Holiday ones.

On Christmas eve, she gave Santa a seductive lap dance that had me holding my cock the entire time. Then someone read a sexy version of the Night Before Christmas, and she acted the whole thing out. She ended that night with Santa coming down the stripper pole while she was hiding under the tree. When he set about putting presents under it, she started being naughty and causing mayhem. He kept blaming the other dancers dressed like elves and spanking them. It was both hilarious and a real turn on too.

On Christmas night, she did a gift-themed dance dressed in bows, peeking in and out of the presents. Opening them to reveal other dancers. The night ended with everyone on the stage singing, "We Wish You A Merry Christmas," as fake snow fell from the ceiling. It was spectacular.

On New Year's Eve, I watched her exit her limo, but she didn't dance, and I roamed all the different Clubs hoping to catch a glimpse of her. It was packed that night, and Jennifer Lopez was rumored to be in the house dancing. I walked through the whole casino with the song by Sam Hunt, "Take Your Time," playing in my head. If I had stumbled upon her, that was going to be my plan—security detail or not. Somehow I was going to make eye contact with her and draw her to me. Then I would let her know that I don't want to change her life. I just want some of her time. I grin. I get to tell her that tonight.

On New Year's Day, there was another birthday boy in the house celebrating his 21st birthday, and while she again wore the gold chains and had him tied to Seary's Hot Seat, her dance was entirely different. The only thing similar was the unwrapping of the chains with her as the birthday gift and those beautiful nipples painted with gold dust. My cock stayed hard the entire night, and in bed, I again dreamed the Wonder Woman dream. Only this time, she knelt in front of me and sucked my cock dry before disappearing. I woke again screaming, "NO!" But I wasn't in a bad place. No panic. Just frustration and sheets soaked with cum from my wet dream.

I arrive at the house and the delicious smell of Maria's cooking. She's in the dining room, setting the table for two when I come in. "Yay! You're here on time!" She sounds more enthusiastic than usual to see me. "Go wash up, and let's eat. I have a date!"

I stop dead in my tracks. "A date?"

"Yes!" She claps her hands together, then starts happy dancing back to the kitchen.

"With who?" I frown and follow her in.

"With a man I met at the grocery store." She giggles. "A tall, dark, handsome man too." She fawns over his imaginary face. "Oh, hell yeah."

"What's his name?" I demand.

She stops, suddenly realizing I'm not happy for her. "None of your business." She puts her hands on her hips and sasses me. "Don't go getting all territorial on me now. I won't have it."

"Maria. I. I. I'm happy for you. It's just as long as I've known you, you've...." Her face makes me stop. "I should stop talking now."

"Yes. You should."

"At least tell me where you are going?"

Her eyes narrow suspiciously. "We're going to his place."

I open my mouth to protest, and she sticks her hand out and then cuts her throat with it. I close my mouth but narrow my eyes at her too. We stare each other down—a war of wills. I speak first. "I could tie you up and keep you here."

She bursts out laughing. "He owns the grocery store. I've known him since the first day I moved out here and went shopping to feed you. His name is Trent Monty. He's thirty-three and a really nice man. Recently divorced with three kids. All of whom will be with us tonight. We're going to take them to the UNLV Runnin' Rebels basketball game. I'll be home before you, but if I'm not, don't wait up." She flips me off as she dances back to the stove.

The rest of our visit is spent eating and discussing our prospective dates. Up until tonight, I had not shared with her who I was going to see every evening these past few months while I was here. When I told her, she whistled and said, "'at a boy! As long as I've known you too, you've never once mentioned anyone either. I knew whoever it was, was someone exceptional. The renovations to the East Wing are very nice. So how did you two meet? Tell me about her."

I laugh, embarrassed. "You probably know more than I do about her. I haven't actually met her. Tonight's going to be the first time."

She drops her fork. "You've been stalking her?"

"Stalking is a harsh, scary word, Maria." I frown at her and smirk. "I saw her dance in November, and she completely captivated me. I fell hard for her then and made this appointment. I've been watching from the audience and waiting patiently for her for three months. Three long agonizing months."

She laughs with me. "I fell for Trent the first time I saw him too. I've been stalking him for fucking years. Talk about frustrating patience." She rolls her eyes.

I pick up my wine glass and hold it up. "To our new flames."

"May they scorch themselves forever on our hearts."

When we are finished eating, we clean the table off together, and I push Maria out of the kitchen, then stand blocking the door. "I'll do the dishes tonight. You get going."

"Ok." She giggles. "No arguing here. Even though I know you'll put them in the dishwasher."

"That's right! Now go!"

I watch her nice ass as she struts out and call

after her. "Wear your skinny jeans." She spanks her ass without looking back.

I go into the kitchen to load the dishwasher. As I work, I sing "Fix" by Chris Lane. I'm going to whisper in her ear. "Baby Girl, I'm what you've been missing. I got your 'fix' right here." Then I'm going to ignite in her a flame that won't go out, make her burn for me. I'm going to make her addicted to me. Umm-hmm. I have big plans for this one.

In the shower getting ready, I let my mind play all the visions of Seary's expressive passion as she dances that have scorched themselves onto it—all these months of watching her. I do feel like a hunter stalking its prey, but in a good way, in a very good way. Soon my arms will be holding her tight. My fingers feeling the soft, subtleness of her tenderness. My eyes seeing the yearning in her eyes for me. My body feeling her body withering under me. My ears hearing her moans and calling my name as she begs me to possess her. Then moaning as I own her completely, pounding her with hard, hammering thrusts until I shoot my cum deep inside her, marking her as mine!

I step out of the shower, and my hard-on leads the way. I grab a towel, dry my hair, then my body, and enter my dressing room. My black tux is waiting for me. Getting dressed, I see my reflection in the mirror and stop to stare. I have a shit-eating grin from ear to ear on my face. Ha! I'm so happy right now! Finally!

I dance out to the garage, slide behind the corvette wheel, crank it up, and squeal the tires as I peel away, feeling young and carefree. In just one hour, I'll be staring into her eyes.

When I arrive, Jimmy trots out and opens my door. "Mr. Moore. You're back and looking very dashing."

I laugh at his choice of words. "Prince Charming dashing?"

"Yes, sir!"

"Excellent." I give him a nice tip and strut my swag ass through the door, heading to the Gentlemen's Club. When I arrive, I go straight back through the dance hall, which is loud and packed to capacity for Valentine's Day, to the VIP area and swipes my card at the security door. The little green light shines, and I turn the handle. My nerves are raw, and I take a deep breath. Entering the hallway, the silence is comforting as I walk down the corridors to find room number 40. Beverly promised it was the largest and had the best acoustics. When I put my hand on the door handle, I hold my breath while I turn it then push it open. The smell of roses and magnolias hits me, and I smile. "Perfect!"

Once inside, I'm ecstatic about the setup. Rebecca has done a fabulous job! There are red, purple, and gold silk drapes hanging on each wall like veils. In the corners are stripper poles, with the fresh flowers woven like vines. In the center of the room is a small table with a purple silk cloth, ruby red dinnerware, and gold tableware. The ice bucket contains a bottle of Moët & Chandon Dom Perignon White Gold Champagne. There are only two chairs in which to sit, tucked under the table. No couch. I wanted to eliminate the temptation of having sex from the room. For these first two hours, I intend to seduce her and leave her wanting Moore. I grin. If she wants to return with me tonight to Red Rock, the East Wing is finished. I'm ready for her.

I check my phone. I have only 5 minutes left. One last time, I review the list I prepared, going over what I want to do. To kiss her hand. To whisper my name in her ear. To watch what makes her smile. To listen to her voice inflections. To watch her mouth move as she talks. To read her body language. Her pulse beating in her neck. Her breasts rising and falling with her excitement. The way her facial expressions flicker with my words and tone. To drink in her light green eyes and seduce her with mine.

I take up post by my chair to wait. I'm ready.

....

....

....

What the hell? I pace in the room. Something isn't right. I check my phone. It's 10 minutes past the hour, but it feels like an hour past.

Then I hear a tap on the door. My first instinct is to say, "Come in." But I know Seary would have. She wouldn't have knocked. My heart locks down tight. I feel cold hardcore steel wrapping around it, and then I hear the pounding in my ears, drowning everything else out. With deep, measured intakes and forced exhales of breath, I gain control, containing my response. I know the pain is coming.

I walk in slow motion to the door and watch my hand reach for the handle. The click of the door latch releasing sounds like a gunshot. Pulling it open, I stare into the face of Beverly.

Her first words confirm my fear. "Mr. Moore. I'm sorry to inform you, but there has been a family emergency earlier today, and Seary has returned home."

I close my eyes as I step back, and she enters the room.

Behind my eyelids, I see fire burning on the stage, as the dancer that has scorched my soul, and know, for the time being, she remains untouchable.

"Is she alright?"

"Yes, she's fine. Of course, you will receive a full refund."

I nod, not the least bit concerned about the money. "Do you have any idea how long she will be away?"

"I'm sorry. No."

"I want to keep the appointment."

She nods. "Very well. As soon as she returns, you'll be first."

I hold my hand out, and she takes it. "Thank you, Beverly. I would appreciate weekly updates to know you haven't forgotten."

She nods, "Of course, I will text you."

And with that assurance, I walk out to fly home to Live Oak, Alabama, to wait for Seary to return to Vegas.

One hour earlier

Siri

The rhythm of my swim stroke calms my mind, quieting the echoes from the gentleman's club.

As I approach the wall, a hand appears, waving under the surface.

What the hell? I stop swimming and tread water.

My best friend and manager stands on the edge of the pool. The look on her face makes time stand still.

"Cat, what's wrong?"

"Siri, there's been an accident."

My heart stops, then starts to race. "Who?"

"Come here, baby girl." She holds up a towel.

Swimming to the stairs, my mind is both blank and racing.

Blank, not wanting to think about how bad this must be for Cat to use her key to my apartment and invade my privacy.

Racing, wondering what has happened to whom.

As I emerge from the water, I ask again. "Who?"

She holds the towel for me. "Come sit down."

Oh, god!

My heart beats hard with a dull ache as I allow Cat to wrap the towel around me and lead me to the barstool in the kitchen.

When I'm seated, she moves to the liquor cabinet, takes two lowball glasses, and pours us both a heavy splash of Crown Royal. Neat, so it bites.

She doesn't say a word until we have both taken a hit of the whisky, then she says one of the two names no one wants to hear. "Your mother..."

"There's been an accident. Your dad called me when you didn't answer your phone. He doesn't know much, but they are prepping her for surgery."

I take the glass of whisky, toss the rest back, then stand. "I need to pack. Will you ask Bart if I may use his jet?"

"Sure, baby girl. I'll make the arrangements."

An hour later, I follow Brutus through McCarran International Airport to Bart's private jet. He keeps looking down at me. I know he's worried I'll lose my shit before I get on board. My hands are shaking like leaves.

When we walk out of the terminal onto the tarmac, he asks, "Are you sure you don't want me flying home with you?"

"No, I'll be fine," I say, braver than I feel.

I take two steps up the stairs, then turn and face

him. "Brutus," my voice cracks, "Thanks for having my back all these years."

He grins, "Siri, don't get all sentimental now. You'll be back soon enough. Your mom's had a bad accident, but she will be fine."

I nod. "I'll call you when we touch down and the minute I know something."

Once I'm on board, I look out the window. The big giant of a man who has been my bodyguard from the beginning is standing at the terminal waving. I wave back, knowing he can't see me in the little window, but I do it because it makes me feel better.

As the jet taxies down the runway, I promise myself as soon as Mama doesn't need me anymore, I'll return home to Vegas. I close my eyes and try to rest, but the tears begin, and instead, I cry. This isn't the triumphant return to Live Oak, Alabama, I had envisioned.

For three years, I've lived a life other people only dream of as the headlining act at Been Jammin', the premier gentleman's club on the strip. As well as Surreal, the star of the strip, an anonymous celebrity impersonator.

I smile. I truly live a life others only dream of.

I close my eyes to rest.

CHAPTER TWELVE

Live Oak, Alabama
One month later

Aurelius

"Moore speaking. Yeah, man, I just pulled into the parking lot at Dogwood Court." My eyes scan the landscape. "It's a nice, high-end apartment complex. Upscale and appears quiet."

I give my Army buddy, Dirk Sam, the skinny on some properties for him and his wife to rent while they are here at Fort Rucker for his advanced training course.

The office door swings open, and a bolt of lightning shoots through me. "What the hell?"

I lower the phone. The most beautiful girl in the world casually walks across the parking lot right in front of me.

I lift the phone, "Dirk, let me call you back."

"Everything all right?" Dirk asks.

"Yeah, yeah. I'm good. I'll call you right back."

"Standing by," he says and discounts.

I can't believe my eyes! Seary is here!

Man, is she ever gorgeous. Dressed in a black business suit skirt with a white button-down shirt, she almost pulls off a business vibe, but there is no way to hide a body built like that. Her breasts strain the buttons of her shirt, and her miniskirt hugs her nice full ass.

All doubt that the effect she had on me in Vegas was nothing more than a passing attraction vanishes. Simply the sight of her sends my heart racing and my cock growing.

She stops next to a customized Shelby GT500 and accidentally drops her car keys, and they land under the car. She doesn't squat. Instead, she bends over and stretches her hand out, reaching to retrieve them. Her ass tilts up, and the hem of her skirt rises. The view hardens my cock.

My god, this girl is perfect!

She stands back up with her keys in her hand and tugs her skirt down to cover her perfect ass. Then she opens the car door and lowers her voluptuous body gracefully into the driver's seat. As she eases out of the parking spot, she glances my way, and a ray of sunlight highlights her face.

She is stunningly beautiful.

I grip the steering wheel and hang my head until the rush of emotion passes and my cock is soft enough to walk.

I call Dirk back. "Sorry about that, but the girl of my dreams just walked by."

"Oh, snap, buddy. Say it ain't so," he laughs.

"Oh, it's so. It is so, so." I chuckle with him.

Two days later.

Siri

The belt moves, and my items slide to the cashier. The little old lady in front of me smiles sweetly and apologizes for taking so long.

Instantly, my impatient mood changes. It is not that big a deal to be a few minutes late. Mrs. Smith, my landlord, won't be upset.

I nod, "God bless you too, ma'am."

Once in my car, I hit the gas to compensate for the lost time on the highway. My hands tap the steering wheel as I absentmindedly rehearse the video of Pharrell Williams' "Happy" in my mind.

I can't wait to tell Cat I intend to do "Happy" for my return Surreal performance. She will come unglued. James may have heart failure, though.

My mom's accident wasn't as severe as I initially thought, and she was good as new within a week, but I decided to take a month off to spend some quality time with my parents.

I'm meeting with Mrs. Smith this morning to inform her that I'm returning to Vegas at the end of the month. The thought of seeing my team again puts a smile on my face.

Parking, I grab my bags and head into the lobby. A Tuxedo Black Metallic Ford F-150 SVT Raptor Special Edition is in the visitor's spot. "What a badass truck!"

Walking through the lobby to the elevator, I glance toward the office and see Mrs. Smith talking to a —stud muffin. His hair is buzzed on the sides, but the top is long, thick, 'dirty blonde' naturally streaked with sun highlights. It's sleek and moving gently as he talks. He's wearing a pale blue shirt with distressed blue jeans, and based on how much taller he is than she is, he's over six foot tall. With his athletic build, he might be pushing two hundred ten pounds.

I announce my presence by clicking my heels on the floor, and Mrs. Smith looks around him and waves. He turns to look too.

My breath catches in my throat. My heart stops beating.

My God! He is beautiful!

Perfectly symmetrical features.

Golden tan skin.

Dark hawkish brows.

Piercing light eyes —rock me to my core.

Umm. Deliciousness.

I enter the elevator and push #9, wishing I hadn't gone grocery shopping this morning and could walk over and introduce myself.

As soon as the doors close, I look up at the ceiling and laugh, "WOW! What just happened to me?" Wild chaos soars through my veins, and I shake my head. I have never reacted like that to a man before, which says volumes because men are my clientele. "That dude was freaking fine!"

When the elevator stops on my floor, I run to my apartment at the end, rush inside, and stuff my grocery bags in the refrigerator. Then I'm right back out, hurrying to the elevator, hoping to return to the lobby before the stud leaves. Wanting to see him up close and personal to verify my reaction was justified.

Pressing the down button, I wait impatiently. Then, as soon as the doors begin to open, I slip through the gap and push the button to close the door, forcing the doors shut without waiting. On the ride down, I position myself in front of the gap, ready to exit when there is enough space. I'm prepared to step out when the elevator bounces on the stop. But right when the doors slide open, the phone alarm I set the day before to remind me of my appointment blasts "When I Grow Up" by The Pussycat Dolls.

"Oops!"

I stretch my torso and shove my hand deep into my front pocket. Trying to pull it out as I step through the gap proves to be a BIG mistake. I stub my toe and trip. My phone clears my pants, and I lose my grip, sending it sailing through the air with the song blasting the entire lobby. I stagger and flail until I regain my footing. Somehow managing not to bust my ass.

Recovered, hoping I didn't look too spastic, but pretty positive I did, I stroll over to my phone cool as a cucumber and bend over to pick it up. As my fingers grasp it, the weight of my thick mane shifts with the change in the gravitation pull, forcing me to reach up and release it from the heavy clip. Instantly, my face is engulfed by my mane. Out of stripper habit, I flip it up and over my head as I roll up.

The song is almost over when I finally tap the music off. "Yeah! Yeah! Yeah! Everyone knows I want to be a star when I grow up."

I attach the clip to my jeans, square my shoulders, and turn toward the office. But my step balks.

The stud is leaning on the door's threshold, completely relaxed, watching me with a sexy smirk.

Oh ... Holy Hades!

My heart and my breath collide in my throat.

My view shrinks.

The rest of the world falls away.

Our eyes lock.

I stare into the most intense gaze on the most handsome face of the sexiest man I have ever laid eyes on and witness his beautiful face smile.

SWEET ZEUS! He looks like a golden god!

My abs tighten, and my tummy lurches hard. It feels like I did a backflip off the high dive. My typically composed, sophisticated Seary, that I have trained so hard to become, is knocked for a loop. I feel my phone slip out of my fingers.

His smile turns to a smirking grin as he pushes off the wall and steps toward me. His eyes are boring into mine.

Rooted to the spot, captivated by his manliness, embarrassed by my response, a shy smile spreads slowly over my blushing face as Siri Wright responds.

"Hi." His deep voice sends shivers through me.

"Hi." My breathy voice answers, and I cringe

inside, unable to control the chaos roaring through me.

Just then, Mrs. Smith comes bustling out of the office, and the golden god stops advancing but doesn't release my eyes.

As soon as she sees me, she asks, "Miss Wright, do you mind if I show this young man the available apartment?"

My response comes out barely above a whisper, "I don't mind."

His light eyes twinkle at me, and from this distance, I can't tell if they are blue or green, but they are smokin' hot!

"Shall we?" Mrs. Smith asks him.

He turns and nods to her.

His profile is beautiful too.

Straight nose.

Strong jaw, but not hard.

The curve of his neck, proud and regal.

She takes off for the elevator, but he turns his attention back on me and walks over. My heart skips more than one beat.

He doesn't say anything. He walks over, bends down, and picks up my phone. My body tunes into his in a way I've never experienced with another man before, and it feels like a million butterflies are soaring inside me.

"I believe you dropped this ... again," he says as he looks up at me.

My mouth goes dry, and my heart stops in shock. The overhead light shines unguarded into his eyes, and they are deep, rich, sapphire blue!

This man is beyond gorgeous!

Dumbfounded, I stare into his peaceful pools as he stands. His aura is magnetic and powerful, and the space between us becomes thick with electricity as he towers over me, dominating me without trying.

He holds out his hand and says, "Here you go."

I force my eyes to look down at my phone cradled in his palm. For a moment, I stare, hesitating. Knowing that when I touch him, the spark will ignite a fire in my soul, and everything will change. Wow, it already has.

I reach for it, and as soon as my fingers touch his, a slight static current pops the tip. His big hand closes over mine, holding it hostage, and a wave of electricity surges into me. With the speed of light, it travels up my arm and down to my clit, producing a pleasurable tingle.

I lift my eyes back to his, and his crinkle like he knows what just happened.

I whisper, "Thanks."

"You're very welcome," rumbles from his chest.

Then he backs away, holding my hand until the distance pulls it from his, and I melt with the subtle signal that he doesn't want to let me go.

Then he turns and walks off to join Mrs. Smith, who has been waiting patiently by the elevator.

Thoroughly enchanted, I admire his retreating manliness.

He is confident but not cocky.

His shoulders are very broad.

His waist is very small.

His legs are straight.

His posture is perfect.

His gait is strong.

He glides with masculine grace.

I watch his ass moving in his jeans.

It is to die for!

My mouth waters.

He is some kind of sexy.

Mrs. Smith leans around his torso so she can see me. "Miss Wright, why don't you ride up with us? You can put your groceries away."

He stops with her words and turns for my answer.

"Yes, ma'am. That's an excellent idea." I manage

not to sound as pumped about it as I am, but my eyes sparkle sassily into his, and he grins at me.

Now, it's my turn to captivate you and take your breath away. I am a lot more than your average sweet southern girl. I walk-trot up the short distance to him, bouncing my braless tits. His eyes fall to watch their fluid dance, and I'm glad I went with an off-shoulder, ruched crop top today. Its form molding design is comfy, but now I'm so happy I chose it because it hides everything without hiding anything.

I stop in front of him. "You don't mind, do you?"

"I don't mind." His honest grin assures me, then he ushers me toward the elevator. "Ladies first."

I smirk hard at that label. It's never a term used to describe me, but I like how it makes me feel. He has no idea I'm a stripper. I strut my Vegas diva stuff for him, knowing his eyes are glued to my ass.

Teasing is what I do best.

CHAPTER THIRTEEN

Aurelius

THE LITTLE MINX is feisty and flirty. We are going to have some kind of fun!

I follow her into the elevator, and she leans against the back wall. I stand close enough to her that I can feel her without touching her, and we stare straight ahead as polite strangers do while Mrs. Smith pushes the panel button.

I can't help the grin that spreads across my face when Mrs. Smith only pushes one floor. Perfect! I can see Seary smiling too. That fact wasn't lost on her either. That's a good thing.

As soon as the doors close, the temperature inside the tiny space begins to rise. I know my heightened, excited state has my body heat jacked up. So when Mrs. Smith says, taking out her phone to text. "It's hot in here. The air conditioning must be broken. I apologize," I smirk and glance down at Seary. She's biting her lip to keep from laughing. She knows why.

I shift my shoulders slightly to watch her as the elevator rises. She glances up at me, and her light crystal green eyes smiling at me in her beautiful face sends a surge of desire coursing through my body again, and my smile is wiped away. She is so stunningly beautiful.

She stares at me, absorbed in my gaze, and I notice the tips of her tits harden and elongate, pushing against the soft lace top, thrilled with my attention. My cock responds in kind, remembering what they looked like, covered in gold dust.

I grin at her, knowing we are on the same wavelength. She takes a deep breath, and they tease the edge of the low neckline. A low moan escapes my throat when my cock thumps, wanting to slide between them.

A satisfied smirk flits across her face, and I grin. She knows the effect she has on men, and she's playing a good game with me.

The elevator stops, and the doors slide open. Mrs. Smith exits, turning to the right.

Seary glances up at me as she pushes her sassy ass off the wall. Touché, babe, I wave her forward. You won round one.

She glides out, turning left, and I follow Mrs. Smith to the right to 9G at the end of the hall. She's blabbing about the furnishings being included, and that's excellent news. I won't have to move any of my shit. I can move in.

While Mrs. Smith unlocks the door, I look back to see where Seary lives. She's opening the door to 9A. But, right before she steps inside, she looks down the hall at me and smiles.

I grin, then follow Mrs. Smith in, not needing to see the apartment, just needing to rent it.

Siri

When the door closes behind me, I lean against it and let the million butterflies flying around express themselves as silly giggles.

"This guy has IT ... in droves! Forget the groceries!"

I rush to the bathroom to check my reflection, and happiness beams back at me. My eyes are twinkling like crazy!

I comb my fingers through my platinum-blonde hair, fluffing it for a sexy tousled Marilyn Monroe look. Then I adjust the ruched crop top for maximum effect.

Returning to the door, I listen for their voices. When I hear Mrs. Smith blabbing, I casually exit.

Mr. Sexy is walking beside her. The shock of how hot he is hits me again, and watching him walk to me makes me tingle.

The fabric of his shirt molds itself on his muscular pecs, and the tailored cut accentuates his trim waist. His distressed jeans are tight on his straight muscular legs and exude strength. The whole package he presents radiates health and vitality.

She calls out, "Come on, Miss Wright. We will wait for you."

He freely gives me a brilliant smile, and my tummy lurches hard, doing a backflip. I hope I never get used to that sensation.

There is something special about the way he walks. I can't quite put my finger on it.

Perfect posture. He's confident but not cocky.

There's something else about his carriage that makes him stand apart from the other guys. He glides gracefully and smoothly, but it is not like a cat. Instead, there is an air of something else.

As he draws closer, his smile relaxes, and he's even more handsome than before. A vision of him naked, looking at me with that expression, becomes a goal.

When our eyes meet, he mouths, "Perfect," and his expression makes me feel that way.

Lengthening my stride so that my tits sway gently to the rhythm of my gait, I work it.

All men love bouncy tits.

His eyes fall to watch them.

When I reach the elevator, I play it cool, avoiding eye contact with him. Mrs. Smith glances up from her phone, smiles, then walks a few steps away to text in private.

Unable to resist, I look into his face. His intense gaze captures mine, but the expression in his eyes surprises me. They are not leering or heavily laden with lust. They are soft and sincere.

Mrs. Smith informs me as she pushes the elevator button, "Mr. Moore has decided to rent 9G."

I hold out my hand, thrilled he's going to be my neighbor. "Mr. Moore, welcome to Cloud 9."

As his beautiful golden hand engulfs mine again, the electricity sparks through me, and I thoroughly enjoy the thrill it gives me.

But rather than shaking my hand, his thumb strokes circles on my skin, and wave after wave of sweet sensation tickles my clit making it pulsate softly.

Damn. Mr. Moore has some serious seduction skills of his own!

The elevator arrives with a ding. Mrs. Smith looks up, puts her phone in her pocket, and laughs. "I've never thought of that. Cloud 9. That is very clever, dear."

After one last satisfying stroke with his thumb, he motions for me to lead him to the elevator.

"After you," he says softly, and I hope that's his intention.

Following Mrs. Smith in, we move to the rear for

the 'hot' ride down. All I can think about is his rock-hard body and whether he wears boxers, briefs, or goes commando.

As soon as the doors close, he shifts his shoulders to study me again. I stare straight ahead, smiling, enjoying his attention.

After a few moments, I cut my eyes to read his expression. He shields the lust there with a smile.

Damn. He is fine!

Mrs. Smith remarks again about the air conditioning needs to be checked, then apologizes to us for the heat.

"It's okay, Mrs. Smith. I am enjoying it." I flirt with him.

He chuckles, and the sound is music to my ears.

Just then, the timer I set to end my meeting with Mrs. Smith goes off. "Wild Thing," sung by The Troggs, blasts the small space.

Mr. Moore's eyebrows shoot up in total surprise.

Without giving it any thought, my dancer bumps her hips to the lyrics' beat. An involuntary half-smile sneaks across his face as his eyes hood, unable to hide the lust now.

Damn, that look. You are one sexy man.

Mrs. Smith glances over her shoulder. "Someone significant, dear? Do you need to get that?"

"No, it's an alarm. Sorry about that." I answer as I turn it off.

As soon as the doors open onto the lobby, Mrs. Smith exits. I take a step to follow, but Mr. Moore reaches out, laying his hand on my arm, touching it gently but firmly.

"Hey," his deep voice says softly, "Is there someone significant in your life?"

I frown, "Excuse me?" I look into his eyes, and they search mine.

"Is there someone significant in your life?"

His intensity surprises me, and the truth in them shocks me. He's worried Mrs. Smith's implication was correct: I have a lover.

I open my mouth to answer but then shut it, wondering why he cares. Then it hits me like a ton of bricks. I'm used to men who hook up regardless of commitments. But he's not a cheater. He's an alpha through and through, and alphas don't share. If there is someone else in my life, he will back away.

My eyes twinkle, and I tip my head, letting my hair shield my face from the lobby. Then looking up at him through my eyelashes, I give him my sweetest smile and tease him, "Not until an hour ago."

His big beautiful smile shines down on me as he chuckles, getting my meaning. I move to stand toe to toe to him and return the question. Making sure he understands moving forward, we are equal. "And you, Mr. Moore? Is there someone significant in your life?"

The elevator doors close, shutting out the world, and there is only us.

He leans forward and softly says in a quiet voice that washes over me from my head to all ten toes. "Not until about an hour and 5 minutes ago."

I start to laugh, then hide my face in my hands, shaking my head. "I must have looked like the biggest goofball ever!" I peer over the tops of my fingers at him. "Can we erase that five minutes, please?"

He laughs at my expression, and the sound is infectious. I giggle as he taps his head. "Nope. Steel trap. Some moves took my breath away, babe."

We laugh as the elevator doors open again, and he waves me out first.

Walking side by side to the office where Mrs. Smith is patiently waiting for us, he asks, "Wild Thang, huh?"

"It's a great song, isn't it? I set the alarm earlier to ensure I didn't get trapped in the office listening to Mrs. Smith tell stories about her cats."

He throws his head back and laughs aloud. My heart sings with the sound of his happiness.

He leans toward me and says with the song's correct voice inflection, "Groovy!"

I lay my head back and laugh aloud too.

When we reach Mrs. Smith, she smiles, "Well, it looks like you two have hit it off."

Neither of us comment. We just smile at each other.

"Mr. Moore, I will have the paperwork drawn up tomorrow."

"I will see you then." He answers her, then turns to me, leans over just a bit to block her, and says softly so only I can hear. "I hope to see you tomorrow too, Miss *Wright*."

The innuendo is clear, and I look one last time for today into those sapphire blue eyes and drink in the gorgeous, golden god's face. Then, I whisper, "Ditto, Mr. *Moore*."

He smiles, then turns and walks away.

I admire the view as I watch him go out the door and climb into the big badass Ford Raptor Special Edition 'real man' truck.

Yes, of course, that is *his* ride.

I turn back to Mrs. Smith. She has been watching me watch him. "He is quite the handsome young man, isn't he?"

"Yes. He is."

When we go inside the office, a resident is crying. Mrs. Smith rushes to her and puts her arm around her. The poor girl sobs in her embrace. Mrs. Smith asks me with her eyes, 'Can we do this another time?'

I nod quietly and back out.

In the elevator, I decide not to text Cat about my return after all. I have some thinking to do.

My life just changed in the span of an hour.

I sure didn't see Mr. Moore in my stars.

Aurelius

When I pull out of Dogwood Court, I'm flying high as a kite. Meeting her ... touching her ... thinking for a moment that she might be with someone else, feeling the devastation, then the relief....

It's over for me. She's the one. I have to regroup. Make a new plan. She's a sweet, southern girl from my hometown. How did I not know her growing up? How did she slip past my radar?

As I turn onto the highway to the farm, I call Ann. Maybe she knows her.

"Sup, Big Brother?"

"Hey, I have a question for you. Do you know ..." I pause, realizing I don't know Seary's first name. "A girl from school. Her last name was Wright."

She asks, "Why?"

I can hear her smirking. "I've just run into her at Dogwood Court, and she's hot as hell. I wondered if she grew up here and if you know her."

She laughs, "What were you doing at Dogwood Court?"

"I went to rent a place for Dirk Sam and his wife, but after seeing her, I rented the apartment myself."

"What the hell?" She dies laughing, and I bust out too.

"It sounds nuts, doesn't it?"

"For you, it sounds insane! But to answer your question, no. I didn't know any Wright's in school."

"Okay, thanks." I hang up before she can grill me further.

Mrs. Smith opens the office at 9:00 AM. For the next ten minutes, I plan my move into the apartment. I'll pack a week's worth of clothes tonight, then swing by in the morning before heading to Rucker to fly, sign the lease and move my clothes in. Then, I will spend the night under the same roof as my future bride tomorrow night.

When I turn onto the drive that leads to the farm, I pass the construction crew on their way out. Earl stops in the road to chat. "We didn't finish the framing upstairs today. We're a little behind schedule. I know I told you we would finish by the end of the month, but we ran into a problem."

I listen as he recaps what happened. Then when he's finished, I let him know there's no rush. He has more time.

"That's a relief. We need it."

"I'll catch up with you next week."

"Thanks, man."

"Sure thing."

When I pass the barn, Flicka and Blue are grazing in the pasture. I had intended to ride today, but it's too late now.

I pull into the garage, hit the remote to lower the door and walk into my grandparent's old farmhouse.

My phone dings. It's a text update from Beverly.

> This is your weekly update as requested. We still do not have a return date for Seary, but we are hopeful it will be soon.

I stare at the text. Yesterday, I would have been annoyed Beverly didn't have a return date yet. Now, I'm ecstatic. The longer Seary delays her return, the better for me. She's on my turf. I'll take her on my terms.

Then a horrible thought pops into my head. What if Seary knows Maximus Moore booked her and has been waiting for her to return instead of getting a refund and rescheduling when she's back?

If she identifies me as that dude, I'm screwed. She will assume I'm stalking her and ruin any chance I have with her. Even if I deny it, the odds are astronomical that we would meet like we did. She won't believe me. I know I wouldn't.

I stare at the text, trying to decide whether or not to ask Beverly how much Seary knows, but I don't want to tip my hand that I've met her. Beverly most definitely will assume I'm a stalker.

I could cancel the appointment, but if I do that, I won't get a heads-up when Seary decides to leave Alabama.

I take two beers out of the fridge and walk outside to the patio to ponder my dilemma further.

Playing Seary this way goes against who I am at my core, but I'm not going to destroy her trust before I've earned it, either. For the time being, keeping my identity secret from her is my only option. I tip the first beer up and drain the bottle.

It's not like I don't know how to keep secrets. My whole life has been segregated into secrets based on who surrounds me at the time. I toss the empty beer bottle into the trash can.

Just when I thought I would be free of deceit, the girl of my dreams walks into my life and nails that door shut. I'll have to play this just right, or I'll screw myself over.

So … I have to maintain my integrity and win her trust while not letting on that I know who she is. Jesus H. Christ. What if I slip up and call her Seary? I tip the second beer up and drain half of it.

How do I avoid making that mistake? I rub the bottle with my thumbs as I think about it. Remembering how her hand felt in mine and how her pulse quickened when I stroked it. Then it hits me, and I smirk, knowing I got this now. "I'll just call her 'Wild Thang.'

I stretch out in the chair and finish off my beer,

dreaming of all the ways I will take her in the future and wondering when I can convince her to go to Rome with me so I can photograph her in my studio.

Then a brilliant thought occurs to me. We won't have to jet halfway around the world to my studio. I'll tweak the renovations scheduled on the East Wing.

Damn, that's perfect! She's perfect! This whole situation is perfect!

Now, to play the hand I've been dealt ... perfectly.

CHAPTER FOURTEEN

Aurelius

I WAKE with a boner fueled by a dream of Wild Thang in a customized playroom. Tossing the covers off, I grab my phone off the nightstand and jot down a few notes inspired by the dream.

The notes include:

- A studio with stripper poles.
- Video recording.
- Black lights and strobes.

- Expand the Roman bath.

Afterward, I turn on the shower, step in and lather up my erection. As I stroke, I let the visions in my dream fuel my fantasy. Jacking off will be a regular necessity. There is no way I will be able to tame the beast while I slowly seduce Seary if I don't keep him drained.

I mean, Wild Thang. I can *not* call her Seary!

I amp up the speed of my stroke as my balls tighten. Then I close my eyes, lean my head back, and repeat "Wild Thang" over and over as my cum explodes. Then vanishes down the drain.

When I'm spent, I lean against the wall, letting the water run over my body and rinse away the remaining sexual tension.

Mrs. Smith walks out the office door as I enter the lobby. When she sees me, she smiles and comes over.

"Hello, Mrs. Smith." I greet her, then laugh at how happy my voice sounds.

"Hello, Mr. Moore. I have a quick errand to run, but my assistant Lucy has the lease ready."

"Yes, ma'am. Thank you." I nod. Then ask, "Mrs. Smith, Ms. Wright wouldn't happen to be home, would she?"

She smiles, "No, dear. She works."

"Oh!" I glance away, realizing that means she isn't intending to return to Vegas anytime soon. I look back at Mrs. Smith. "I was hoping to see her today."

"Well, she usually arrives home around 4:15."

I nod, disappointed. "I'm going to miss her then. I have to be on the flight line at 5:00."

She smiles, "I'll let her know you asked about her."

"Thank you. I appreciate that."

When I enter the office, a small Asian woman is standing in the doorway of Mrs. Smith's office, so I introduce myself. "Hello, I'm Aurelius Moore. You must be Lucy. We spoke on the phone before about renting an apartment."

She nods curtly, then steps back into the room. I follow her in and sit on the chair in front of the desk. She doesn't smile at me. Instead, she slides the paperwork across the surface and says with a thick accent, "Read carefully."

I pull it to me and scan the pages, then I scratch through Dirk's name and pen my own on the line, sign it, and slide the lease across.

She frowns. "You rent? Not you buddy?"

"That's correct." I nod as I stand to reach into my pocket, pulling out a wad of cash.

She watches me count out the deposit and first month's rent, then when I hand it to her, she asks, "Why you, not him?"

I shrug and give her my player grin. "I met Ms. Wright yesterday."

Her eyes narrow, and she wags her finger, saying, "You flyboy. You leave her alone. She lady. She sweet. She work. She home alone. She good girl. She no party girl."

I am shocked speechless by her reaction. But I keep my cool, and as I reach for the key on the desk, and respond simply, "Yes, ma'am, I won't cause any trouble."

She stands and glares at me as I back out of the office. Then, right before I turn my back to her, she says again. "You leave alone."

On the way to my truck for my duffle bag, I chuckle at Lucy's protectiveness of Seary. She just confirmed my impression in Vegas was correct. Seary's a good person, and now I know for sure she's a sweet, southern girl.

I grin as I lift my duffle bag full of clothes out of the bed of my truck, then the cooler with a few essentials for the refrigerator. Lucy's going to be disappointed because there is no way in hell I'm letting this wild thang run free. I'm going to tame her, then claim her.

Siri

The entire day at my temp job, I think of the Golden God and wish I wouldn't have gotten so bored being home and taken this job to pass my time while my mom recuperated. If I weren't obligated to be here, I could be at the apartment helping Mr. Moore move in.

But I only have a few more days. Then my stint is up. I smirk, and I'll have more than enough time to reel him in.

When 4 o'clock rolls around, I hit the door with a smile. I've decided I'm going to give him a housewarming gift.

At Publix, I walk through the doors with purpose and direction. The cashiers all know me, and Janice, who is in the express lane today, pokes fun at me.

"Siri, back so soon? Weren't you in here yesterday? Did you forget something?"

"I am out of wine, and I came in too early yesterday." I laugh and joke with her. "I forgot alcohol isn't sold on Sunday until one o'clock. It's like y'all are in the Bible Belt or something, so I had to swing by on my way home tonight."

"Yeah, I foll-a ya. I guess Sin City stays open and turned on 24/7?"

"Yes, it does. You should come out and try it sometime. You might not come home for years either."

"Yeah, right. I am not going to hell." She blurts out before she realizes she's condemned me. "Sorry, Siri. I will say a prayer for you."

"It's okay, Janice. I'm not offended," I answer in the awkward tension between us now.

She focuses on my items. "And the cookies? What's up with the junk food? I thought you were a total health food nut."

"Yeah, well. They are a gift for a friend." I laugh. "Don't look so shocked. Not everyone has shunned me. I have friends here." After a dramatic pause, I roll my eyes. "Okay, only one, but still."

She laughs with me, "I'm your friend, Siri."

"Great! That's two," and the awkward moment is over.

When I pull into the parking lot around 4:30, I search for his black Raptor, but it isn't there.

"Well, hell!" I sigh, feeling deflated. "I'm not getting a Golden God fix tonight."

The next morning at work, I call Mrs. Smith at 9:00 sharp to get some information on Mr. Moore from her.

"Mrs. Smith, this is Siri Wright in 9A."

"Oh, yes, dear, are you calling to reschedule your meeting?"

"No, ma'am. I'm calling to get a little intel on Mr. Moore."

She chuckles. "I have to protect his privacy, but I'll be happy to try to answer. What would you like to know?"

"His haircut suggests he's in the military."

"Yes, he's active duty. Stationed at Fort Rucker. He's a helicopter pilot."

I grin, "That's dope."

She chuckles again, "He sat in his truck a long

time before he left. I suspect he was waiting for you to come home from work as long as he could."

"I hate I missed him. So, that means he's already moved in?" I bite my bottom lip. *Did we sleep under the same roof last night?*

"Yes, he did. He is quite smitten with you, dear. He originally called to check out our apartments for a friend of his that is coming in TDY. But one look at you ...." She puts her hand over the phone and speaks to someone who just entered her office. "I'll be right with you." Then she asks, "Is there anything else you would like to know? Someone just came in."

"No, ma'am. That's all. I just wanted to know if he was military and when he was moving in."

"Okay, well, let me know if you think of anything else. I'm here to help."

I laugh at that. "Thank you, Mrs. Smith. I appreciate it."

Siri

When I whip into the parking lot, it's 4:10. I drove like a bat out of hell to get home. When I spot Mr. Moore's badass truck parked in front, an excited uncontrollable squeal emits from my mouth. A parking spot next to it is empty, so I whip right in.

Rushing into the lobby, I glance at the office and see Mrs. Smith standing in the doorway. She smiles and waves then points upstairs and gives me the 'ok' sign. I dart into the elevator and push #9. As the doors close, I show her my crossed fingers.

She nods, grinning.

Nothing like having a spy on your team.

When the elevator doors open, I casually step out and look down to 9G. Mr. Moore isn't in the hallway, so I sprint down to my apartment, throw open the door, begin stripping as I race to my closet, throw on a cute loose-fitting tangerine outfit that's made of ultra-soft thin cotton that drapes over my curves seductively, and slide my feet into a pair of pearl flip flops. Then I rush into the kitchen, throw the plate of cookies into the microwave for a minute to heat, place a kitchen towel in a basket, and when the microwave dings, I take the warm plate of cookies, set them inside the basket, and cover them with the towel. Hooking the basket on my arm, I grab the bottle of wine and float gracefully down to 9G.

At his door, I push the towel off the cookies letting their aroma fill the air. After several deep breaths to calm my nerves, I raise my knuckles to knock. But before I make contact, Mr. Moore pulls the door open. He takes two steps, then stops, surprised to see me standing there. Then his big beautiful smile spreads over his gorgeous features like sunshine peeking out from behind a dark cloud, and his deep voice rumbles like summer thunder when he greets me. "Miss Wright, I missed you yesterday."

Holy Hades! He is hotter than I remember! How is it possible one man can be this good-looking?

The light from the hall shines in his sapphire blue eyes and on his sun-streaked highlights like a halo shining over his dark blonde golden goodness.

My tummy lurches so hard I almost pee my pants, but thankfully all the years of wearing a professional poker face comes to my rescue, and I manage to keep my composure.

I look past him into his dark apartment and ask, "Is this a bad time?"

His eyes devour me, causing my tits to harden and push against the soft top. I wait a moment for him to respond, but he doesn't say a thing, so I look at him, smiling, teasing him.

His expression makes my panties wet. Desire plays openly across his face as he takes his time observing my unannounced presence.

As he studies my outfit, the basket on my arm, and the bottle of wine in my hand, I study his face in greater detail. His dark, almost black, angled brows accentuate his eyes to perfection. His white teeth stand out against his tanned skin and are perfectly straight. His lips....

Sweet Zeus, how could I have missed his lips? They are sculpted perfection. Full ... sensuous ... and I know they taste delicious. I lick my own, and his eyes dart up to my mouth.

The trance-like state he was in vanishes, and he playfully inhales the scent of the cookies. He says as he turns the lights back on, then pulls the door all the way open, gesturing for me to enter. "Of course not. Please come in."

When I walk in, I pause just inside the door and turn to face him. He reaches for the basket, and his hands brush my skin, making me tingle there. He lifts the basket from my arm, and takes the wine out of my hand, then walks to the kitchen.

Following him, I enjoy the spectacular view. His

flight suit accentuates his v-shaped physique and frames his killer, coffee-bean ass.

In the kitchen, he sets the basket down and says, "I'm sorry, but I can't enjoy a glass of this fine..." He holds the wine bottle away so he can read the label. "...Merlot. I'm flying tonight, but I'll give you a rain check." He sets it on the counter next to the basket of cookies, then gestures to one of the barstools so I sit. "I will be happy to devour these delicious morsels with you now, though. Would you like a glass of milk?"

Without waiting for my answer, he grabs two lowball glasses and the milk from the refrigerator, then pours us both a glass. I marvel at how comfortable and relaxed he is and how I feel the same way with him.

He pushes a glass to me, and I pull it closer. Then, he reaches into the basket, takes a cookie, dunks it in his milk, and then plops it in his mouth ... whole.

My breath pauses, watching him, mesmerized. Damn! There is something about the way he moves that turns me on. He's sensual and so sexy! His mouth works over the cookie with his eyes closed, enjoying the moment....

Sweet Zeus, this dude is doing it for me.

When he swallows, his Adam's apple shifts, making my mouth literally water. His lips slowly begin to part, spreading over his straight white teeth in a sexy-as-hell grin as he moans, "Yum."

My thoughts exactly! I lower my face to stare at the counter, trying to get my desire under control. I take a deep breath, hold it, then let it out slowly.

Then I lift my eyes to his, and my tummy tightens. His lids are hooded, and the desire I see on his face sends a jot of pure passion coursing through me.

He smirks, knowing what he's doing to me. He picks another cookie up. "Have one. They are delicious."

I lick my lips, reach into the basket, pluck one out, and then stare at his cookie as he dunks it. Mesmerized, I watch it travel to his mouth, and when he sends more of his tongue out to greet it, my clit says, 'well, hello there!'

Then he lays the cookie on his thick flat tongue and slowly pulls it into his mouth. A wave of desire crashes over me, causing my eyes to hood.

He nods at the cookie in my hand and says, "Your turn, Wild Thang. Eat up." His tone, his smirk, that name, and his eyes all tease me, challenging me to turn him on too.

I lick my lips and grin as my eyes twinkle into his. *Challenge accepted.* I hover my cookie over my milk and wait for his eyes to shift from my face, then my tits, to the cookie.

I dunk in my milk in a rhythm that matches our thoughts, and the milk dances in the glass. Then I lean forward, opening my mouth to engulf it, pressing my tits on the counter, and lift my eyes to stare into his.

The passion in his eyes makes me wet. I know what he is thinking, and it isn't how good that damn cookie tastes. It's how good that would feel to his cock and how deep can he shove it down my throat.

When I swallow the cookie, I let my own 'sexy as hell' smile spread slowly over my teeth and acknowledge, "That *was* delicious!"

Siri

His dark eyes bore into mine for several seconds, turning my flirty confidence into something much more primitive that matches his. I feel a door inside my soul unlock.

Then he smiles that sexy half-smile and challenges me again. "Would you like ... more?"

We stare at each other with the innuendo heavy between us. I drop my eyes to stare at my milk, not really seeing it. I can feel him watching me, looking for my answer.

He smirks, thinking I'm hesitating, but I'm sizing him up. How far can I push him before he loses control? I glance at him. I really want you, Mr. Moore.

Swinging my hair so it is all on one side, I look up at him from under my lashes and reel him in. Reaching for the cookie, I accept the unspoken challenge saying, "I do want more."

His expression changes. His hungry eyes wanting me —watch me.

As I hover the cookie over my milk again, my eyes assure him you are never again going to dunk a cookie without seeing this replayed.

I wait while his eyes travel to the cookie, then I

dunk it in the milk with such force that it sloshes over the rim and slips down the glass.

His breathing changes.

I push my tits down onto the counter again and pucker my lips, then suck the milk from the cookie.

His breathing gets shallow.

You weren't expecting that, were you?

Then I arch my back, thrusting my tits toward him until my neck is fully extended and exposed. Sticking my tongue out and opening wide, I insert the whole cookie into my abyss. Then I close my mouth and swallow the entire thing.

His breathing stops altogether.

My eyes twinkle, teasing him as I reach for the glass and lick the spilled milk off it. I turn the glass until it's licked clean. Then my tongue darts around my parted lips, licking the milk off them too. Then I suck my fingers clean.

I hear a very low, primal groan emit from him. Then, laying my head sidewise as I look up at him, knowing that image is burned forever in his mind, I smirk. "They are to die for."

His hooded eyes and his hungry expression were nothing compared to the dark look on his face now.

I freeze. I have pushed him to the brink.

For all my experiences in Vegas, I have never

seen this expression before. I've met alpha males, but I've never met a hunter. His intensity is truly as frightening as it is exciting. I can see and feel the ferocity of his passion as he fights the beast inside.

Sweet Zeus! That expression. I should be afraid. But I'm not. The electricity sparking between us sends my hand to reach for his, and his eyes dart to it, then they look directly into mine. The piercing power touches something deep inside me, and I feel my monster stir.

My tits swell with the pounding of my heart, wanting to escape my bra. My skin flushes. My clit throbs to life. A hunger deep inside stirs. His look turns me on in a way I never thought possible. He is a beast who would feast on me, and I want him to.

But he groans a low moanful sound as he gains control and reins his desire in. Closing his eyes, hanging his head, he leans on the counter for support, and I withdraw my hand.

Under his taut flight suit, I watch his big chest expand and contract as he breathes in and out, controlling himself, and his arm muscles bulge with the tension. The counter blocks my view of his erection, but I know he's hard.

Staring at him struggling, I wonder how this intensity between us can happen so fast. I have no idea, but we have not only undeniable chemistry but a passion between us!

Slowly, his expression subsides, and his muscles relax. He shakes his hanging head and chuckles softly. The sound is gentle but not vanquished.

When he lifts his face to mine again, the corners of his eyes crinkle as he grins shyly. Realizing he has shown me a side of himself few see. He says, "Damn, woman."

My heart starts to sing. He's so cute!

Grinning back at him mischievously, I reach for another cookie. His eyes flare slightly, and I see a trace of concern flash across his face.

I smile sweetly up at him and wink. Don't worry. I'm not going to push your buttons again. Not yet, anyway. I hold the cookie out to him. "I've had my fill of cookies. They were delicious. Have another."

He laughs as he takes the cookie. He stares at it for a moment, then dunks it in his milk. "Are you from around here?" He opens his mouth and unceremoniously stuffs his gorgeous face as he waits for my answer, relaxed and comfortable again.

"Yes and no. I'm complicated."

"No doubt." He rolls his eyes, making me laugh.

"And you? Are you from around here?"

"Yes and no too. I'm complicated as well." He flirts, mimicking me.

"No doubt." I roll my teasing eyes right back at him.

He takes two more cookies and stuffs his mouth, so I answer his question. "I'm actually a dancer."

"I know. I've been dreaming about you ever since I saw you."

"I'm surprised you could tell I was a dancer in that first five minutes your steel trap won't forget."

He chuckles, then stares at the basket, thinking. "Yes, well... well I..." He puts his hand on the basket, then smiles. Taking two more cookies, he says, "There was a very dramatic dance move in that 5 minutes."

I talk with my hands. "Let me guess. It was the impressive way I managed not to bust my ass?"

He laughs and shakes his head. "No, actually, it was the way you flipped your hair and the way certain parts bounced that stuck with me." He stares at my tits. "Pretty amazing move." He looks into my face and smiles. "You are unforgettable."

"Mmhmm." I glance down at her glass, resisting the urge to confirm that's how the bloggers describe Seary.

"So, what are you doing this weekend?" He asks.

"Nothing. Why?" My face tilts so my eyes can dance for him.

His reflect mine. "I was hoping we could share the wine one day."

"That would be nice. I would like that." I bat my eyelashes.

His voice drops an octave, growing serious. "Listen, I hate to, but I have to go."

I smile, satisfied I've teased him enough for one day, and slide off the barstool.

"Finish your milk." He commands, and I obediently pick the glass up to drain it but decide to make a toast first. Lifting it, I wait for him to raise his. "Here's to ... Moore."

His smile is like a magnet on my heart. He clinks my glass with his. "Here's to ... Wright."

Our eyes twinkle into each other's as we finish off the milk. As soon as I set my glass down, he scoops it up and quickly washes it. Then takes the empty basket, and we walk together to the door.

CHAPTER FIFTEEN

Aurelius

As we walk down to the elevator, I ask, wanting to see if she will be honest with me. "So, where's the 'no' you are from?"

She tips her head confused, so I clarify. "Where does the complicated dancer live?"

"Oh," she smiles, then looks down, thinking. "Vegas." She answers truthfully, cutting her eyes to catch my reaction.

"Awesome. Vegas is one of my favorite places in the world." I assure her.

"I don't usually tell folks from here that. Not because I am ashamed because I'm not. I love my life." She shrugs, "But because they can't handle it. You know, Sin City. To them, Vegas is the capital of Hell." She shakes her head, then looks into my eyes —open, honest, and direct. Something deep inside me responds. "It is really rather sad to me. I pity them as much as they pray for me. I'm the one who doesn't judge others. I'm the one who actually loves everyone, no matter who they are or where they come from or how they choose to live their life. I'm the one who values honesty above lies. But in their eyes, I'm the one going straight to Hell."

Her answer stuns me, and I half turn to look at this unique person walking beside me. Before I think about it, I share my thoughts with her, "You are such an interesting find."

She smirks and half turns to me too. "Now, how sad is that? Honesty is interesting. No, even worse, honesty is a find?" She bumps into me playfully as we walk, and the intimate move jars that deep spot inside me again.

She's so real. She doesn't wrap herself in fake pretenses.

The urge to pin her against the wall and kiss her until she wants me as much as I want her enters my mind for a fleeting moment, but then it flees in the face of my guilty conscience. She thinks she's as big a stranger to me as I am to her.

"So, where is the 'no' you are from?" She asks me, expecting me to be as open and forthcoming as she was. I realize if we are going to have a future together, I have to be completely honest with her about my life and hope that when the time is right, and I do confess my deception, she has fallen so deeply in love with me that she will forgive me.

I lower the facade most people see and answer. "I grew up as an Army brat, and now I'm an Army aviator. I fly Apache's. I've lived in Live Oak the longest, so I call it home, but I have family in Italy too, and I bounce back and forth from here to there."

"I've always wanted to go to Italy, particularly Rome. I love architecture and the arts." She says as we reach the elevator. "Thank you for your service too."

Her sincerity pierces me again. She isn't saying it because it's the accepted response to say to those who have volunteered to serve and protect our country and our freedom. She says it because she means it, and it humbles me in a new way. While harsh memories from the wars and the battles I engaged in flash across my mind, her sincerity gives me an appreciation for my service on a whole other level.

And as the door of my heart swings wide open, I tell her the truth. "You're worth it."

My answer stuns her, and for a moment, we stare at each other, connecting on a spiritual level. Something I have never done with any other woman. Then she smiles softly and says, "You are also an interesting find, Mr. Moore."

Then, knowing my time today with her is coming to an end, I push the down button, then turn around and hold the basket out. She reaches for it, and when she pulls it toward her, I use her momentum to invade her space. Needing to feel her against me, I lean down to whisper in her ear. "Thanks for the cookies."

Her breath pauses as I dominate her, then she whispers back, staring at me. "You're welcome."

I drink in her light green eyes, framed by dark, thick lashes, and tease her. "I enjoyed watching you enjoy them."

Her eyes twinkle, and I feel the thrill of them in my heart. "I enjoyed watching you ... enjoy watching me ... enjoy them."

I chuckle. She's sharp. This one. "Did you bake

them yourself?" I ask, not caring, just wanting to stay in the moment.

"Ha, no! I can't cook." She laughs, easing the sexual tension building between us. Then she confesses, "Compliments of the bakery in Publix."

I hold my position and her eyes. "Your honesty is refreshing, you know."

She drops her eyes from my intensity. Then she looks up from under those thick lashes. "So I've been told."

The elevator arrives with a ding, and my time is up. I lean close, inhaling her scent, and whisper the truth. "I will be dreaming of the way you eat cookies for the rest of my life, and I can't wait to see what you will do with the wine."

Then I back into the elevator holding her eyes captive, and she says, "I can't wait to show you."

My cock hardens with the promise, and I blindly push the lobby button. As the doors close, I state the truth. "You are more than I dreamed of."

Her pleased expression sends a spark of pleasure through me, and in the last shrinking span, I share my Italian side. "Ciao, Bella."

Siri

Trying not to swoon with his words, I hold my breath as the elevator doors touch. Then I sprint to my apartment, fling the basket on the counter, and rush out onto the balcony. Bracing on the rail, I lean over it, waiting for Mr. Moore to come out.

As soon as he exits the building, he turns to look at my apartment, and I wave. He grins, pleased, and throws his hand up. Then the Golden God stud walks with his perfect posture and strong gait to his truck. When he pulls the door open, he gives me another wave, then he gets in, closes the door, and cranks the engine.

As his truck backs out, I wave again. I want Moore!

When he's out of sight, I go back inside and put away my groceries, then take a salad out to eat.

I think about what just happened between us. When something as innocent as eating cookies and milk turns into combustible sexual tension, there is no denying the physical attraction. I've been working as a stripper long enough to know that the kind of chemistry we have is rare. It's spontaneous. Effortless. It's incredible and undeniable. The kind that causes passion. But there is more to Mr. Moore. I'm not quite sure how to put it.

I take my salad out onto the balcony and plop down in a chair to eat. A hummingbird flitters around, then flies off. I stand and walk over to the edge of the railing, looking for it in the flowers that line the sidewalk leading to the walking trail cut into the woods surrounding the complex.

Tomorrow afternoon, I'll leave work thirty minutes early and run on the trail, then be outside cooling off when he comes down. It won't look staged.

My phone sings "Amazed" by Lonestar. I snatch it up to read my mom's text.

Arrived safe. Excited. Boarding the boat. Will check in when I can. Don't worry.

OK. HAVE FUN! BE SAFE!

DADDY AND I LOVE YOU, PUMPKIN!

LOVE YOU TOO!

I smile at my phone. My parents are always on the go. As soon as the doctor cleared her, she booked a sailing trip around the Virgin Islands for them. She said if she was going to have to rest, she might as well do it on a yacht. "You need to get back to Vegas, Siri. I worry about you being gone so long from your dream job."

Aurelius

That was a close call! I would never have invited her in if I'd known eating cookies would be such a turn-on, but ... goddamn! Everything about Seary is sexy.

I turn right out of the private drive and head to Fort Rucker for my last night as a flight instructor.

As soon as she stood in the doorway with the basket of cookies and wine, her sweet southern personality beaming at me, I knew I couldn't turn her away. I had to invite her inside. She might have taken my not inviting her in as my not being interested in her.

But damn! She pushed me hard, nearly too far, and I almost lost control. All I could think of was snatching her up by her beautiful headful of hair, ripping her pants off, slamming her little dancer's body down on the counter, and thrusting into her with every ounce of power I possess.

Not waiting until she willingly offered, but pounding her, ravaging her. Not gentle and slow, but hard and forceful. The kind that, without consent, can be misinterpreted.

I have never forced myself on a woman, but I'm not always gentle, and I wouldn't have been right then. All I was thinking about was taming that tail and claiming her as mine.

I wipe my hand down my face to clear away the stress.

The expression she was wearing.... She was as turned on as I was.

Jesus, that was a close call.

Hell! I shake my head again. I *want* her to wear that 'take me now' expression when she looks at me from across a room full of people. I want her to look at me, knowing I have claimed her and knowing she is mine.

But relationships aren't my thing. That's why my call name is Hardcore. I flash back to the day I was labeled.

Dirk bragged to the others on the flight line one Monday morning.

"Dudes, my wingman Aurelius earned a new nickname Saturday night."

"Spill it!"

"His new name is Hardcore, but I call him Hard for short."

They all laughed at that. "Cause his dick stays hard all the time?"

"Well, that too, but no. Hey, Hard, come over here and tell them what happened Saturday night."

"Naw, man, let it lay."

"Oh no!" They all chimed in. "Come over here and spill it!"

I waved them off, but they all walked over while Dirk began telling the tale.

"We walk in, right? And immediately, the Hulk here draws the ladies' eyes. You can hear the word 'Eye Candy' buzzing around the bar."

"That's two words, Dirk."

"Shut the hell up, Aurelius! Don't be so technical all the time." He turned his back on me. "Anyway, we sit down at a table and nothing happens, right? Wrong! Some drunk chick comes up, plops down in his lap, and starts to grind him."

"No, she didn't. Quit exaggerating."

"You're ruining the story, brah." He said over his shoulder.

"Get it right then."

"Ok. She didn't grind him, but she did plop down in his lap."

Someone else chimed in. "Shut the hell up, Aurelius. Grinding is better."

I threw my hands up. "Fine. She did grind me, but it wasn't immediately."

They all laughed.

"But our Officer and a Gentleman here, being the best wingman ever, simply stands up and excuses himself, leaving me the drunk chica. When he comes back, I've made a move to hold her right here on Sam-I-Am!" He pointed to his junk and they all laughed.

"But her wing-lady rescues her, and they leave." He frowned, and everyone booed.

"Which should be bad, right? Wrong! That's good because she broke the ice, and now Mr. Muscles there is acting like a chick magnet. I swear they were swarming around him."

He stopped talking and looked at his biceps. "Maybe I should improve my guns." Then he flexed them, and they popped up. "Naw. They're awesome too."

Everyone laughed.

"By the time last call comes around, I'm working my tail off to pick one up to take out to the parking lot, and stud there is working his off not to have a threesome at the table."

"Did he end up going hardcore on them like the dawg he is?"

Someone chanted. "Who let the dawg out?" So, of course, everyone barked.

"Naw, brahs! He mowed them down! It was brutal, I tell you!" He hung his head, then shook it. "He told them fine foxes, 'Look! I'm not into you, and I'm not getting "in" to you.'"

"Ahhhh!" The guys all moaned.

"That's a hardcore rejection right there."

"Thus, his new call name." Dirk proudly declared.

I sigh. Damn. I have no idea how to have a relationship. I pull into the stage field. But she's a stripper, so going slow isn't her thing, either. As long as the sex is good.... I know how to please a woman. I calm down and exit the truck.

As I walk across the parking lot, I hear Jeremy call out, “Hard, wait up!” I turn around, waiting for him to catch up. “So, you're leaving us? Tonight's your last night?”

“Affirmative.”

He offers his hand. “You'll be missed.”

I shift my helmet and my flight bag to my other hand to shake it. "Thanks, man."

"You got any plans around 5:00? I need a favor."

I laugh, "AM or PM?"

He laughs too. "PM."

"What 'cha need?"

"I need a body for B-ball. We're playing for a spot in the post-playoffs, but Larry's wife went into labor a little while ago, so he's out. Can you fill in?"

"Sure," I smile, knowing this will successfully keep my hands off the sexy stripper one more night.

"Thanks, buddy." He pats me on the back. "Are you any good?"

I laugh, "Yeah, I'm good."

"Excellent!" He nods, then says as he backs away. "Wear a white teeshirt with your name stenciled on it and blue shorts."

Siri

"Brick House" by the Commodores goes off as I slip between the sheets. I lift my phone to read Cat's message.

Hey, baby girl! Just checking in. Do you have a return date yet?

No. Something's come up. Actually, someone has shown up. I've met a man!

Tell me!

He's my new neighbor and he's gorgeous!

Sweet! And convenient! :) What does he do?

He's a helicopter pilot.

Military men are HAF! Have you hooked up yet?

Not yet. We just met.

Well, don't overthink it. Have a little fun. Damn, I have to run.

Ok. Miss you! Give everyone my love.

I will. Laters

Drifting off to sleep, I flashback to how I met

Cat. *It was in September. Piper, my British roommate at Florida State and my best friend, and I were walking down the Vegas strip, heading to work at Coyote Ugly, when she slipped her arm around me and pulled me in tight. "Siri, I meant to tell you earlier, but I kept chickening out. I'm going home."*

I stopped dead, and she continued on a few steps, then turned around to face me. "Home? As in, back to England?"

She nodded, walked back to me, put her arm around my shoulders, and turned me back toward Coyote Ugly. "Yes, I miss my Mum and the rain." She teased me in her British accent, which she rarely used anymore. "We've had a great run this summer, but I've been away too long. It's time to take my American education home."

"When?" I pouted.

"Next Wednesday."

"Damn, I'm going to miss the hell out of you." She squeezed my shoulders tight, and I slipped my arm around her waist.

"We will stay in touch, love. We are 'soul sisters' after all."

I cut my eyes at her. "You promise?"

"I promise."

We walked a little further before I said, "Well,

I'm not ready to return to Live Oak, Alabama, and the hicks from the sticks. I'm going to stay right here in Vegas until I'm sick of it."

She laughed. "As long as you are dancing, you will never be sick of it. Which is why I signed you up to try out for an opening at Been Jammin's."

I stopped again, "You did what?"

She laughed as she immediately returned to get me. "I signed you up to try out. You're good enough to dance there, and you'll make enough money. You won't need another roommate."

"When?"

"Tomorrow, so don't drink tonight. You're wasting your talent dancing on a bar. It's time you move up to bigger and better things, and I don't want to worry about you here without me."

The next afternoon we entered the Gentlemen's Club with fifty other girls. Everyone was wearing skin-tight clothes and varying degrees of platform heels. Cat walked out onto the stage dressed as a dominatrix. She stopped, surveyed the room, then said, "Welcome, ladies. This is an open call tryout for dancers. But listen up, dancers at Been Jammin' are required to work the stripper pole. If you don't have the experience, don't worry, we will train you. But be aware before we begin, you will dance practically naked. We don't want to waste anyone's time."

I grinned at Piper because she knew I had been dying to learn how to dance on a pole, and stripping down to a thong, topless, wasn't a big deal. Americans consider it slutty, but that's how European women sunbathe on the Beach.

She grinned back. "You'll make more in tips off the pole alone than our entire paychecks at Coyote Ugly."

Cat walked over to the closest stripper pole, touched it lightly, lovingly, and said, "Let me give you a taste of what we will expect from you."

The song "Brick House" by the Commodores started to play, and for the next few minutes, we watched fascinated as Cat dominated it.

More than a few girls backed out, knowing they didn't have what it took.

When Cat dismounted, she said, "If you aren't up to learning to do that, then leave now."

Another few girls walked out.

Piper turned and hugged me. Her keen eyes searched mine. "Siri, you get up there on that stage, and you show 'em what you can do. You show them how unforgettable you are."

I nodded and swallowed the lump in my throat. I

wasn't nervous to try out. Music always makes my body move. I can't help it. It's just something I do. I dance. But I was nervous because you never know what kind of talent they are looking for, and I desperately wanted to be chosen. However, I knew that no matter how well I danced, I could still be rejected based solely on my appearance.

I'm Caucasian, but my skin tone isn't white. It's a soft bronze. I look like I've been in the tanning bed, but it's just my natural color. I'm petite and very curvy with full double D tits and a nice big booty to match. I'm not tall or short. I'm 5'5". My natural white-blonde hair and light crystal green eyes reflect my Scandinavian heritage. My mom always told me I had Mermaid hair because it's thick and wavy. Now, people tell me I'm beautiful, but when I was young, I was bullied.

I stepped up onto the stage and looked out over the tables where the audience sits. The venue was huge, and I realized I really wanted this. I belonged up here, entertaining people. It's what I was born to do.

I looked at Piper, and she gave me her best smile, along with two thumbs up.

Cat snapped her fingers. "Line up, ladies. When the music starts, I want you to dance."

The twenty or so girls left, and I formed a single line. Cat snapped her fingers again, and "Dance For You" by Beyoncé began.

While the other girls began to freestyle, I waited, getting into character. I visualized Beyoncé's music video, then lifted my arms as if I were her, standing in the doorway, looking at my lover sitting on his desk in his office. I channeled Beyoncé and danced the choreography precisely as she does in the music video.

When Beyoncé walks forward to the man sitting on the desk, I walked to Cat and dance up on her. Then I grooved back to the line and continued dancing the routine. Several of the other girls moved in beside me and danced with me.

As the song ended, I strutted my assets back up to Cat and ended it staring into her eyes.

She grinned, "Now, that's what I call dancing."

I smiled, knowing I won that round, then got back in line.

The next song was "Circus" by Britney Spears. Again, I got into character and danced the video precisely like Britney. Not a twitch, a twirl, a hair flip out of sync.

Cat folded her arms and watched.

As soon as "Circus" ended, Britney's "I'm a Slave

4 U" started, and I danced it too. By the time it ended, Cat had made up her mind.

Ten days later, Piper was gone, and I sat in Bart's office in Been Jammin's with Cat, waiting for him to join us.

When he walked in, I was struck by the immediate dominant vibe he gave off, and I wondered if he and Cat have a private BDSM club too.

He walked up to my chair and towered over me. "So, you are the gold mine?"

I couldn't help but laugh. "Cat keeps saying that I'm going to make us all rich."

He laughed and walked behind his desk. "We're already rich." He winks at Cat, and she winks back. "You're the girl that's going to make us filthy rich!"

I grinned as Cat spoke up. "Siri has agreed to the terms of her contract with some exceptions." She smirked at me.

His head tilted, curious.

"She will become Seary, our new headlining stripper, with the understanding that she will not provide our clients with anything more than erotic dancing in the VIP rooms."

He turned a piercing gaze on me. "You mean to tell me you are refusing the extracurricular activities that go along with stripping?"

I answered. "I'll give them lap dances, but I have one hard rule."

"What is it?"

"No touching."

He blinked in surprise. "No touching? Are you serious?"

I nodded. "I'm a dancer. I'm not a whore."

He looked at Cat. "And you agree to this?"

She smirked as she shrugged. "She's that good, but there's more."

"I can't wait to hear it." He leaned back in his chair, cocked a skeptical eyebrow, put the tips of his fingers together, and waited for the mic to drop.

"I want to headline with a full production crew so Been Jammin' can compete directly with the other shows on the strip."

Both eyebrows raised. Then he cut his eyes at Cat, and she nodded. "I've heard her ideas, and they are solid gold."

"But that's not all I want to do."

He frowned, "Go on."

"We all know that Jennifer Lopez danced in the crowd at the other nightclub, and what a sensation that caused. People still go there with the hope that she might return. What if JLo, Britney, or even Beyoncé came to Been Jammin unannounced and

danced to one of their music videos? Do you think people would flock here in the hopes that the stars will pop in and perform when they are here?"

His lips pressed together, and his eyes narrowed.

"This is my idea. We set up the stage just like the music video, then raise the curtain without any announcement. It will be a surprise performance. I will impersonate the star with prosthetics and custom costumes and dance to their video. Since the crowd isn't told anything, they will assume the celebrity performed."

"On the first performance, the actual celebrity will come out dressed in costume to take a bow. Then I will join her on stage, and she'll introduce me as the actual performer, giving me her blessing. We will perform another video together, proving I'm as good as she is. We pay them royalties."

"Each performance after will cause a buzz. Who danced? The celebrity or me. Your customers will flock to Been Jammin's because there is a chance they can witness a surprise performance by a celebrity. But either way, they will be entertained."

His lips curved down, impressed. "You want to be an anonymous celebrity impersonator?"

I nodded. "Yes."

"How?" He looked me up and down.

I smirked. "After midnight, when the crowd is drunk or high, it'll be easy to fool them."

"No, how will you make the crowd love you and not be disappointed that they didn't experience the celebrity?"

"I'll wear a custom costume and perform a pole routine that will take their breath away. I'll have the most talked about tits in Vegas."

He chuckled. "I like it. It might just work."

"One other thing, my impersonator stage name will be Surreal."

"Surreal? Why?"

"Because the performances will be either fact or fantasy, and that's the definition of Surreal."

He nodded. "Okay. You got it."

He stood and shook my hand, while Cat said smugly, "I told you this girl was a gold mine."

CHAPTER
SIXTEEN

Aurelius

When I pull into the parking lot of Dogwood Court, the sun is just coming up. There's an empty spot next to Seary's car. I smirk. She drives an expensive, custom-detailed sports car that will fly down the road. It's not a car you buy off the lot of a dealership. It's a special order, which means not only does she have money, but she has good taste. If she ordered it for herself, it shows she values worth and enjoys the nicer things in life, but she's not flashy.

She didn't pick a Porsche. She chose a fast car which tells me she likes pushing the limits.

I smile. I like pushing the limits too.

Before I get out, I set the alarm to wake at 2:00. Since I didn't pack a stenciled teeshirt, I'll have to drive back out to the farm and grab one. Then get back here before she gets home from work so I can casually meet her in the lobby before heading out to play basketball with the boys.

Siri

Walking down the empty corridor, I think about knocking on his door. I'd bet my right arm, he sleeps in the buff. But I don't. I continue into the elevator. As soon as I walk out into the parking lot, a little thrill surges through me. He's parked right next to me.

When I enter the office, there's only a minute to spare, but no one notices. The two executives who are in my area, Charlie and TD, have been away this week on business and are not in yet. When they arrive a few hours later, they have on golf shirts.

Charlie greets me, "Good morning, Siri."

"Morning. Did y'all have a successful trip?"

"Yes, we did." Charlie replies, then winks at TD as he asks me, "Did you miss us?"

TD chimes in, "Of course she did. Right?"

I roll my eyes at them as sarcasm drips from my "Mmhmm."

Charlie, who considers himself a serious playboy, is tall, dark, and handsome. He is physically fit and a stud by most standards. He grew up in Live Oak, graduated college, moved back home, and has worked here since. He enjoys pleasing women and would be a regular in Been Jammin's VIP lounge. The girls would love him because he would be a big tipper.

Thomas David, TD for short, just started working here a couple of weeks ago and has a serious 'bro' crush on Charlie. TD's a West Coast transplant. He's short but cute. His personality drips with what he thinks is charm. He has deep blue eyes. Thick hair that's too long, and often wears it in a man bun. His teeth are slightly crooked, but he bleaches them, so they're less prominent. He's never played sports, or lifted weights. He's a wormy, spoiled, rich, pretty boy. A total metro man complete with a tanning bed tan and manicured nails. Which in Live Oak isn't normal behavior for a man. He would also be a regular in Been Jammin's VIP lounge, and the girls would love him too for his big tips, but he would be cocky, throwing around his money for attention.

Thankfully, the phone rings. "Run along, you two." I turn my back to them and answer it as they go to their offices.

It's Charlie's young wife, who I expect isn't in her twenties. "Siri, hey, this is Mandy." She whispers, "Don't tell Charlie I called. I want to surprise him. Is he in yet?"

"Yes, ma'am. That's right."

She giggles, "Good. I went shopping and have a new outfit to show him."

"He will like that."

She giggles again, "Is TD in too?"

"Yes, ma'am. That is correct."

"Good. My outfit will make his eyes pop out of his head." She giggles so hard she can barely breathe.

I chuckle despite my professional attitude. "He would enjoy that very much. Will you be stopping by later on to demonstrate your products?"

"Oh, you are good, Siri. Yes, I'm on my way now.

Charlie was gone five whole days! I need a good fucking."

"Yes, ma'am. Please don't describe it to me. Save your sales pitch for him."

She giggles again, "I like you, Siri."

"Likewise, ma'am. See you soon." I hang up the phone and doodle a pretend note.

Mandy pops in from time to time to do Charlie in the office, but when TD joined our staff, that dynamic changed.

Charlie introduced TD and then took Mandy into his office. They weren't exactly quiet, and when she left, TD opened his office door to watch her.

When she walked out the glass front door, she turned to face TD, winked at him, and made the invitation.

TD walked up to the door to watch Mandy with her newly acquired big tits on full display. She lowered herself into her baby blue Mazda Miata. Then she picked them up and arranged them so she could drive away. When she was gone, TD backed away from the door, looked at me, and said, "DAMN."

Then Charlie strolled out of his office to the area water cooler, poured himself a cup, sipped it slowly, then turned to give TD direct eye contact. The unspoken message exchanged between them was meaningful. Charlie wants to watch Mandy and TD. Then Charlie returned to his office with a knowing grin, and TD went to his office with a boner.

I look for Mandy's Miata to pull in the lot for the next hour, but she never shows.

The phone rings, and I answer it. "Connors Chemical Corporation. This is Siri. How may I direct your call?"

"Siri, this is Mandy. My mom stopped by. I won't be coming in this morning after all."

She sounds like she has been crying. "I'm sorry to hear that. Is there anything I can do?"

"No. I just wanted you to know. Thanks."

Hanging up the phone, I stare at it, concerned. She is always so happy and bubbly. To think she has been crying breaks my heart.

Suddenly, Charlie snatches open his office door, and as he hurries out, he tells me, "I won't be back today. Something unexpected has come up."

A few hours later, TD comes out of his office in a full-blown panic.

"TD, what's wrong? Is it Mandy?" I put my hand to my heart.

Deep in his crisis, he doesn't hear me. He paces back and forth and rants. "You can't cancel now!

There isn't enough time to find someone else! Dammit!"

He stops, chews his manicured nails, then starts pacing and ranting again. "The cocktail party is tomorrow night, and you dump me the day before? That's just like you, though, leaving me high and dry!"

He pauses, runs his fingers through his hair, and asks himself, "What am I going to do?" Then his face whips my way, and I shrink from his aggression. He marches over, puts both hands on my desk, towering over me, and asks. "What are you doing tomorrow night, Siri?"

"No," I answer automatically.

He throws his hands up frustrated, spins around, and sits on the edge of my desk, thinking. Then he turns back around, leans over gently, and begs, "PLEASE! I am desperate here! I have to have a date. I can't go alone. It's a couple's thing, and I don't know anyone else in this hell hole I can ask. Please?"

Dammit! He has tears in his eyes. I hate to see a grown man cry. I hate to see anyone cry. I take a deep breath, and my gut screams NO as I give in. "Okay, I will go, but only as a colleague."

"Oh, thank you, thank you, thank you!" He rushes towards me.

"Whoa, whoa, whoa. STOP right there." I throw my hands up to block him.

He stops his advance, then runs his hands under his hair, fluffing it as he regains his composure.

"I have one rule, though."

"Okay. I can handle one rule. What is it?"

"Rule #1: No touching!"

He blinks, then laughs. "I thought you were going to say no drugs."

"You won't be doing that either, but no touching is a hard rule for me. Deal?"

"Deal." He sticks his hand out for me to shake.

I raise my eyebrows. "Really, TD? No touching means NO touching. None, nix, nada, null, zero on the touching."

He covers his chest with his hands and backs away, playing the charming misunderstood douche. "No foul!"

"TD, don't underestimate me. No touching means *no* touching, and I will enforce it."

He laughs, "Got it." He spins away on his heel, taking off to his desk.

I shake my head. This is *not* a good idea. I glance at the clock on the wall. It's 3:30 —time to go. I transfer the phones to the answering service, and I am out of here.

Aurelius

At 4:15, I step out of the elevator and look around. Seary isn't in the lobby, so I head to the door. Looking through the glass, I see her, and I stop to watch.

She's bent over with her hands on her knees, taking deep breaths. The sight of her makes my dick hard. She's dressed in form-fitting black short shorts and a bright pink compression shirt that's so tight her big tits are smashed.

When she looks up, she sees me standing there, spying on her, and she smiles and walks up. Her skin shines with the moisture of sweat, and her face is flushed from running.

Her hair is pulled up into a high ponytail, and instantly I remember her bouncing down the runway in gold chains with her ponytail playing around her face. She was stunning then, but now, she isn't wearing any makeup, and she is simply beautiful.

She pulls the door open, walks through, and a

warm fuzzy feeling spreads over me. I smile. She makes me feel young again.

She looks me up and down as she walks up. Noticing the fact that I'm not in my flight suit and enjoying the view as much as I'm enjoying hers. When she invades my space, the intensity between us sparks.

When she stops, she smiles. She's as turned on as I am. "Hi," I say and chuckle at my lack of conversation.

Her beautiful smile and twinkling eyes tease me. "Hi there. Looks like you are heading out."

"That's affirmative. I have a friendly game of basketball with the bros on post." I look her up and down and state, "Looks like you had a good run. You look hot."

Her head tilts slightly with my words, registering that was a compliment rather than an observation.

So I continue, "You're in great shape. I bet you have great stamina." My sideways grin flirts with her. "Being a dancer."

She looks down, then out into the lobby, then back at me, grinning, "I do."

Then she says, "I run at a pretty good clip for a girl too. I bet you couldn't run off and leave me." She punches my arm playfully, and when it bounces off because it's hard as hell, a flash of desire reveals itself in her eyes, and it lights me up.

I take a step toward her, wanting to pull her into my arms but only daring to capture her eyes. I assure her, "I would never run off and leave you."

All pretense of playfulness vanishes from her face as she feels my desire for her.

I lower my voice and let her know. "If you decide to ... run ... with me, I promise to hang around."

My eyes bore into hers, trying to touch her heart and caress it with my sincerity while not overwhelming her with my dominance. She bites her bottom lip, and hell, it turns me on even more.

Throwing caution to the wind, I ask, "Would you like to come?"

Her teasing eyes flash that she intends to cum, but then she quickly looks away and flirts. "Maybe next time."

I reach out and touch her arm. Her breath catches, so I stroke her with my thumb. Goosebumps pop out and make me smile, knowing just my touch does that to her.

"Walk me to my truck then?"

She looks back up at me and says softly, "Sure."

I grin but let her go. She walks to the front door,

and I follow. She reaches for the handle, but I reach around her and pull it open first.

Once we're outside, I make small talk. "Did you have a nice day at the office?"

"It was okay." She laughs and grins up at me. "Tomorrow's my last day."

I feel my frown fall over my face before I ask, "Are you leaving Live Oak?"

She smirks, pleased by my reaction. "No, just the job. I'm going to hang around here a little while longer, I think."

A grin splits my face. Ah, she's working me.

"Glad to hear that. I thought for just a second you were going to announce your return to Vegas."

We stop in front of my truck. "Not yet. There's a bottle of Merlo and a raincheck to cash before I decide when I'll return." Her eyes focus on my lips, and I see the longing in them. She wants me to kiss her.

I reach out and take her hand, unable to help myself. Needing to feel her. As soon as I touch her, her 'take me' look blatantly stares me down, and all pretense of going slow with her vanishes. I pull her into my arms, unwilling to control myself with her hunger inviting me.

Then my phone in my pocket plays "Same Love"

by Macklemore. Her eyebrows shoot up in complete surprise, and the spontaneous spell is broken. I release her and take a step back, but my eyes remain locked on hers.

As I take my phone out of my pocket, I explain, "My sister is calling." Then I answer it. "What, Baby Sister?"

Ann reminds me she needs my help. "Yes. I'll be there on Saturday." I roll my eyes, and Seary laughs. "I love you too."

I hang up and stuff the phone back into my pocket. Knowing I should go but not wanting to, I look at her Shelby GT500 and acknowledge her choice. "You own an extraordinary car, Wild Thang."

She laughs at my nickname for her and follows me as I walk over to the car.

"Most people don't realize that I drive an extraordinary car. They only see the Mustang body style."

"I'm not like most people." I cut my eyes at her, and she smiles, feeling my truth. "This baby has a lot of muscle under the hood." I stand, reaching for her hand again.

"I assure you, I can handle it." Her eyes drop to my crotch as she takes my hand, but this time she resists my gentle pull to step into my arms.

"Do you drive it fast and furious?" I ask, letting my eyes devour her, trying to convince her to let me hold her again.

"Sometimes, I scream down the highway." She smirks but doesn't budge.

"And other times?" I give her only a half-smirk and squeeze her hand gently, asking for permission to hold her.

"Other times, I like to take it nice and slow." She makes it clear how she wants to proceed.

My eyes hood out of respect for her, shielding my hunger from her.

She relaxes and purrs, "Making it moan."

Staring into her eyes, controlling my desire, I can't stop my need to stroke her hand to let her know my intentions with her are honorable. She looks down, and I squeeze her hand again. "Oh, absolutely."

When she lifts her eyes, they challenge me. I pull her firmly into my arms, not accepting no for an answer. "Wild Thang," I lower my lips, intending to touch hers gently, and she turns her face up to receive my kiss.

But then my phone sings again. This time the ringtone is "American Soldier" by Toby Keith.

The sobering look that comes across her face

startles me. She went from horny to respectful in a split second. I reach up and trace my finger down her face, knowing the moment is lost but knowing I gained more than a kiss would have given me.

I smile at her. "I'm going to have to take a raincheck on that too."

She smiles sweetly, then takes a step back, and I let her go. Pulling my phone back out of my pocket, I answer it. "Moore speaking."

Not taking my eyes off her beauty, I listen to Captain Rhinehart confirm that I am attending the Hail and Farewell ceremony tomorrow night at the Officer's Club on post.

"Yes, sir. I'll be there. Twenty-one hundred hours. Out here." I hang up.

She smiles and says, "My calendar is clear on Sunday."

I grin, "Good. Mine is too."

My phone dings with a text message alert. "That's Jeremy confirming I'm on my way to the basketball game."

She grins and shoos me away. "Go. We'll hook up Sunday."

My grin splits my face with her choice of words, and I confirm, "Def on Sunday then."

She walks around to the front of my truck as I

walk to the driver's door. I climb in, crank it, then roll the window down as I ease out of the parking spot. Pausing one last time to look at her before I pull away, she says, "Your truck suits you. It's a 'real man' truck."

I give her a big smile and a head nod, "See ya, Wright."

She waves, "Ciao, Moore."

CHAPTER SEVENTEEN

Siri

When I arrive at work on my last day, TD is waiting for me. He opens the front door. "I have to go to the other office today. There's an issue I have to handle. Let me have your digits. I will pick you up around 8:30. Where do you live?"

"Dogwood Court. I am not giving you my number. You can message me on Facebook if you need to. Otherwise, I'll meet you in the parking lot."

He presses his lips together. "Fine. The attire is semiformal. Wear something sexier."

I put my hands on my hips and give him a severe smirk. "Go before I change my mind."

He opens the door, takes a step out, then backtracks. His charm is on high. "Thanks, colleague, for doing this for me."

I nod. "You're welcome." And my gut adds, I hope I don't regret it.

As I pull out of the parking lot of Connors Chemical Corporation for the last time, I thank my lucky stars that I went to Vegas and became a dancer instead of an accountant.

When I pull into the parking lot at Dogwood Court, I'm disappointed the Raptor isn't there, but I go up to my apartment to eat and get ready for the cocktail party, knowing I have a plan to see the Golden God tonight.

I grab a chicken salad from the fridge and water from the pantry and go to the balcony to eat. As soon as I step out, I hear the deep hum of his truck and walk to the edge of the railing

The spot next to my car is taken, so he finds another, but he finds one closer to the building. When he gets out, he glances up at me, and I wave.

He gives me a big, beautiful smile and a sexy head nod that causes that sweet lurching sensation.

He is so fine!

He's wearing a big-armed, black tank top over a pair of plaid shorts and flip-flops. The view of his golden hair, broad shoulders, perfect skin, and perfect ass makes me want to say 'screw it' to the cocktail party tonight. But since he also has somewhere else to go, I might as well help TD out of a bind. If I time it right, I can surprise Mr. Sexy on my way down and ensure he thinks of no one else but me all night.

He leans over the side of the truck bed, then stands up with two bags of groceries and a case of beer.

Ah! He's been to the grocery store. He cooks too! This guy keeps getting better and better. I watch the man of my dreams walk into the building like the Golden God he is.

Knowing better than to open my apartment door to catch a glimpse of him, I eat.

Then go back inside, throw away my meal, and grab my laptop. I haven't updated my Facebook fan pages in a while, so I take it back outside to check-in. Whenever I see all the pictures my fans post of how much fun they are having, I'm reminded of how fortunate I am. I truly live a life other people only dream of.

Without an incredible support team that makes everything run smooth, Surreal wouldn't have the nearly 750,000 fans, nor Seary the 300,000 fans. I need to do something special to show them how much I truly appreciate all they do on my behalf. Maybe I will fly everyone to Colorado for a few days this October when the Gentlemen's Club shuts down for the week.

I drop an email to Cat to that effect. Before I close my laptop, I quickly search for Moore, but he doesn't pop up, nor does his sister. I let it go for now and head to the shower to get ready.

As I dry off, I decide which dress I will wear.

If I didn't intend to run into Mr. Moore, I would choose the simple black dress, but because I am, and I want him thinking about me for the rest of the night, I decide on the gold micro-fiber single form-fitting piece of fabric that has a choker style collar and is adorned with tiny gold chains. It doesn't expose much skin but doesn't hide my assets, either. In fact, it has the opposite effect. The thin, nearly sheer fabric accentuates both my tits and my ass.

I decide to wear my hair up in a French twist with little wispy ringlets hanging down. I apply a light brush of silver with a tad of smoky navy at the corners of my eyes. That will be enough to make my green eyes pop, but not so much I look like I intend to make an impression. Wearing theatrical makeup for my shows has given me insight into highlighting my features and an appreciation for wearing as little as possible when I'm not performing.

I slip on my gold chain sandal stilettos. When I examine the effect in the full-length mirror behind the door in my bathroom, the woman who stares back has an air of elegance, and I'm confident I can push Mr. Moore's buttons while presenting a cool, aloft persona at the cocktail party.

I give myself a wink of approval, then walk into the bedroom and head for the closet.

There is no way I'm going off with TD without protection. Brutus will never forgive me if I don't heed his training. My gold Gucci purse has an extra-long, thin strap that hangs nicely with the weight of my Ruger LCR and will go with this dress nicely.

When I open the purse, I discover $3000 in a money clip from the last time I carried it. I toss in my driver's license, then reach under my pillow for my pistol and drop it inside.

At 8:20, I stuff my phone and apartment key in my purse, sling it on my shoulder, and head out.

Walking down the hallway to the elevator, I feel like the Vegas Diva I am for the first time since my return home.

Focusing on 9G, I try to will the Golden God to come out now, so I can strut for him. But I make it to the elevator without his appearance.

I plan to hang out in the lobby and wait for him to show up, knowing he will come over to speak when he sees me. Then, I will formally introduce myself, find out what his first name is, and leave a lasting impression on him that will guarantee he won't be thinking of anyone else at whatever event he is attending tonight.

As I lean forward to push the down button, my purse swings forward, and the weight of it is too heavy to wear safely, draped loosely on my shoulder. The elevator dings, the doors slide open, and I step in. I push the lobby button, then lift the purse strap, and ease my head between the chains, being careful not to mess up my hair. With it firmly in place, I turn to face the front, rolling my shoulder around, testing it. The weight of the gun and my phone makes it hang nicely at this angle.

The doors start to close, so I step back against the wall. When the gap is less than a foot wide, a golden hand slides in between and grabs a door firmly. Both my heart and the elevator doors jolt to a stop.

The sight of his hand sends my heart racing, remembering how hot he made me in the elevator the first time we met.

The Golden God is going to ride down with me!

I hone in on his fingers, thrilled, and instantly turned on. They are long and strong. His nails are clean and neat. It's a working man's hand. I smirk—a real man's hand.

As the doors reverse their path, I roll my eyes upward. *Sweet Zeus, thank you!*

When the gap is big enough, a cooler, undoubtedly full of the beer he bought this afternoon, enters the elevator, followed by the most beautiful man I have ever laid eyes on.

Tonight, he is dressed in a short-sleeved, dark purple J-Crew shirt that's loosely buttoned and tight, white pants. The color complements his golden skin tone.

He is completely distracted, reaching into his front pants pocket to retrieve his singing phone. The tune this time is Dos Gringo's "Has Anyone Seen My Wingman?"

He doesn't see me. He is seriously preoccupied with his phone. He thinks he's alone.

He completes his text, pushes the L button, then his hand brings his phone around, and as he shoves it in his back pocket, my eyes feast on the golden skin of his curved back where it meets the perfection of his full ass.

Damn! That is a perfect thrusting muscle!

As the elevator doors close, I inhale deeply, trying to be as quiet as a mouse, but then ... Oh My God! His cologne! He smells like Heaven itself!

I close my eyes as they roll back into my head and try not to swoon.

Aurelius

The elevator starts its descent, and I step back from the panel to set the cooler down. My eyes catch a sight that startles me and then takes my breath away.

Seary is standing in the corner looking like a fantasy come true. Her hair is pulled up, exposing her slender neck. Her dress is a work of art. It's like a thin gold cloud shielding her nakedness. There are little tiny chains woven through it, binding it to her curves. Her dainty feet are strapped into a pair of familiar gold-chained stilettos.

Instantly, I see her dancing down the runway in nothing but tiny gold chains, and immediately, my cock goes rock hard. The memory brings a smile to my face, and it slowly slides over my features, knowing Seary is trapped in here alone with me.

I turn to face her. Her eyes are closed, and her face is tilted upward. She has a look of ecstasy on her face. I have never seen a more beautiful creature in all my life. She is stunningly perfect.

Savoring this moment, I step around the cooler to stand a couple of feet away from her. I start at the bottom of her gorgeousness and ravage her with my eyes. I want her to feel my possession as they travel up her incredible body. Letting her learn her first lesson. That I can own her before I even touch her. Seducing her mind, devouring her beauty, I take my sweet time and enjoy the journey.

Her shapely legs shift, and my heart starts to hammer in my chest, knowing she's tingling from my dominance. At the line of her short hem, the playfulness I first felt is replaced by a need to conquer. I can see the triangular shadow created between her thighs.

I lick my lips, wondering if she is naked underneath and how sweet she tastes.

I take a step closer and fight the urge to test her wetness now.

She stops breathing and her abs tighten, giving away her clit is throbbing.

Her chest expands, holding her breath, and her taut nipples elongate against the sheer fabric, teasing me to touch them.

The pounding of her heart is so intense her tits pulsate, and the thin fabric rebounds with each ripple. She gulps a deep breath, quivering with excitement.

My cock throbs in my jeans as a low primal growl escapes my throat. My hunger to have her threatens her.

I lift my arms to keep touching her, afraid the spark of her touch will ignite a fire I can't put out, and I'll take spread her legs and take her right now. Pinning her against the wall, I study my prey at my leisure.

She closes her eyes again and takes a deep breath. She should be afraid. But she melts.

The primal moan escapes my throat again, and her eyes hood, watching me with that 'take me now' expression.

I tilt my head and lean in down to smell her essence while letting my eyes caress her neck and then her face.

She studies my ecstasy in her essence, and her face flushes with lust.

I examine her pouty lips, wanting to kiss her so bad. She licks them, and the sight of her wet tongue, then the wetness glistening on her lips, damn near sends me over the edge.

My eyes bore into hers, and she stares bravely, boldly back with both defiance and submission.

That look sends me closer. Crowding her space, towering over her, I lean down, testing the waters, ready to crush her lips with an all-consuming kiss. She inhales my breath, and I swear, she nearly swoons.

My cock begs me to unleash him, but instead, I stick my nose in the nape of her neck, inhaling her sweet scent, then blow a thin line of breath in her ear.

A low throaty moan escapes her, then she turns her face away, biting her bottom lip, and I realize she would flee if she could, but only because she wants to be taken so badly right now.

"Look at me," I command her.

She lifts her face, then looks me in the eye.

A smile eases across my features, and my heart relaxes. She is mine!

I begin whispering, and she studies my lips as they form my Italian words. "Giorno e notte sogno solo di te."

Her eyes flash wildness, and I stare into her eyes. Wild Thang, we want the same thing!

Then the elevator dings, shattering the silence and bounces to a stop. Reality returns and I literally growl my displeasure at being interrupted. But I release her and roll away to the side.

Siri

"Oh...." A surprised voice says into the elevator as we face the front, staring straight ahead. Both of us struggling to gain control of our passion.

I'm breathing in short excited pants. He's taking deep, long, even breaths.

A middle-aged man enters, but his wife takes one look at me, then looks at Moore. Her eyes fall to his groin, and she reaches out for her husband's arm.

"We will wait for the next one." She tells her husband as she pulls him back out. "Herb, come here. Come back out."

The man grunts and tries to pull his arm away, but she wins, and he retreats.

When the doors shut, we don't move, knowing the moment has passed. Then he asks, flirting, but his voice is still deep from his passion. "I guess you are going out tonight?"

"How could you tell?" I sass him.

He chuckles and turns to study me. "With someone special?"

"No." I laugh. "The someone special in my life is going somewhere else." I tilt my head and pucker my lips. "Where exactly are you going?"

He chuckles again, pleased with my answer. "I'm going to a Hail and Farewell on base. I'm obligated to go."

"You mean you're being honored?"

He smirks, "Not exactly, but I have to attend." Then he closes the distance, and his scent fills my nostrils. He smells so damn good!

"Where exactly are you going looking like a million bucks?" His tone is passive-aggressive.

"I'm attending a company party."

"You look hot as hell in that dress."

I grin, thankful I ran into him.

"Scorching hot, to be more precise." He traces his finger down the side of my face, and my abs tighten as my clit thumps, reminding me a little while ago, we were contemplating doing the deed in the elevator. "You know, I don't even know your name."

"It's Siri." He blinks, surprised. "Like Apple's Siri."

"Hmm," he moans.

I ask him, "What's yours?"

"Aurelius." He answers.

I grin. "Aurelius ... huh?" I repeat it, letting it dance off my tongue. "You are literally a Golden God," I smirk at him.

His eyes crinkle with amusement at my reaction to his perfect name. Then he presses his erection against me, pinning me against the elevator wall again.

The elevator bell dings announcing our arrival. He backs off, then waves me out of the elevator first. I exit a few steps into an empty lobby, then turn to wait for him. He picks the cooler up, and we cross together. My heels click on the floor as I strut my stuff, and he glides with masculine grace by my side.

I'm struck again by how comfortable he is in his skin. He doesn't exude confidence exactly. Although I'm sure most people misinterpret his air to be cocky. It's something more like complete mastery. He is supremely competent.

"Aurelius, huh?" I ask, enjoying his name immensely.

"Affirmative," He answers, giving me that big beautiful smile again.

"Aurelius suits you."

He winks.

Damn! That wink is killer!

At the door, he extends his stride so he arrives first. He pulls it open for me, and I float through.

There are a couple of ladies walking up, so he continues to hold the door open for them as well. They tell him, "Thank you," as they enter.

He responds with, "Yes, Ma'am."

He's such a nice guy. I smirk, but there's a bad boy in there that the military has taught discipline to.

Aurelius

Outside, the security lights are bright, illuminating the area. Siri walks so close to me that my sleeve keeps brushing her arm. Then she playfully bumps me.

"So, Aurelius, how long have you served in the Army?"

"I gave them six years, but I'm not a lifer."

"Are you getting out then?"

"Yeah, yesterday was my last day flying. I'm officially on leave at midnight tonight while my paperwork is processed."

"Do you already have plans for what you'll do now?"

I grin at her. "I have a business to step into."

"Oh, what kind of business?"

"I'm an investor."

"A real estate investor?"

"Among other things."

"Hmm," She analyzes me for a few seconds, then she asks. "Do you think you will miss flying?"

"No, I have my private pilot's license."

"Oh, that's cool! Maybe you can take me for a flight sometime?"

At the curb, she steps off, but I pause, waiting until she looks back at me. "I think that soaring with you is definitely going to happen."

She bites her bottom lip, and her eyes twinkle at me. That is definitely going to happen.

A grin spreads across my face as I step off the curb and join her. When we step past the car in the visitor's spot, I look down the row and see a guy casually smoking a cigarette, sitting on the trunk of a candy apple red Porsche, parked seven cars away. He's wearing a dark blue sport coat, medium grey trousers with a light pink shirt unbuttoned for comfort, no tie, and dark brown loafers. His long hair is in a French braided ponytail.

I stiffen and pause, staring at him. I feel Siri 's hand touch my arm, and she leans around to see what I'm looking at.

The dude glances at us, thumps the cigarette into the parking lot, and mouths, "Sup?" He throws in an 'I think I'm cool' head nod that only amplifies he's a douchebag. Then he dismisses us as he pulls another cigarette out of his pocket and lights it.

Siri groans, "French braided hair? Really?"

I look down at her, and she rolls her eyes. "My colleague."

"How well do you know him?" I stare back at him, wondering how he managed to get her to trust him and if I should go down there and threaten him so he knows I'll beat his ass if he hurts her.

"He's new here."

I snap my eyes back to look at her, concerned she has accepted a date with a man she doesn't know very well, and I say so. "You don't know him?"

She smiles, "No, I know him. You don't know him."

"So, who is he?"

"His name is TD, and we've worked together the last couple of weeks. His date canceled on him at the last minute yesterday, so I agreed to fill in."

I frown at her. "Why didn't he just go alone?"

She shrugs, "He said it was a couple's thing."

I frown harder. "What kind of party did you say this was?"

"A cocktail party. That's why I'm all dressed up." She smiles, then twirls around for me, trying to ease my concern, and I'm reminded she's a stripper from Vegas and probably more than capable of handling the likes of him. "I can handle myself. I got this."

"Where do you work again?"

"Worked." She corrects me. "Connors Chemical Corporation."

I frown again. Under normal circumstances, I'm sure Siri could handle herself, but this isn't normal circumstances. I pull my phone out of my pocket and send a quick text to Darren to confirm my suspicions.

Is there a swinger's party tonight?

But I say to her, "Give me your digits. If you get in a bind, I'll come get you out of it."

She smirks, "Don't you mean, 'Let me give you my digits?'"

I smirk. "Let's exchange digits. I'm ready." I wave my phone at her.

She laughs and gives them to me. I send her a text, and her phone in her purse confirms we are now connected.

"Do I have to be in a bind to call you?" She teases me.

I grin, "Of course not."

"Walk me to my truck?" I stall her, wanting to hear back from Darren before letting her go off with TD.

"Sure."

At the truck, I lift the cooler and set it in the back. Then look over my shoulder at her. Yep, she's checking out my ass.

Our eyes connect, and the desire in them assures me that I am the man of her dreams. Wanting to make damn sure that I am the only thing she thinks about the rest of the night, I push off the truck and walk up to her. Crowding her space.

She doesn't flinch. She stands her ground.

I move in so tight my shirt teases her breasts, and they elongate, pushing out to touch me.

She inhales a deep breath and closes her eyes. My scent turns her on. I smirk. Our chemistry is explosive. I study her face and realize she is quivering again.

Smiling with that knowledge, I command her, "Look at me."

Her gaze doesn't get past my lips, so I tease her, whispering, "Sei la donna dei miei sogni."

She sways slightly, then lays her hand lightly on my chest, pushing gently to keep the slight gap between us safe. I smirk, and capture it, then drag it down my torso to hold by our side. I can see the excitement shining in her eyes.

"Don't push me away," I command her again. She bats her eyes, surprised at my tone, but instead of being pissed, she melts into submission. My cock thumps, hardening. Her eyes hone in on my lips. "Translation, please."

"Siri," I pinch her chin, holding her captive, and tilt her face to mine. She squeezes my hand and brings her other one up to rest on my waist.

In complete control, I tilt her face gently until she's

staring straight up, and her arched back presses her tits into my chest. She leans forward, giving in to the feeling and staring into my eyes. I wait until she's longing for my words, then I say, "You are the woman of my dreams."

Her eyes glaze as she hears deep in her soul what I'm saying. With each breath I take, I blow my essence across her face, and I become her whole world. I see her falling for me.

I lean closer, vanishing the gap between our mouths, and her breath gets shallow as mine caresses her lips.

She waits for my kiss, but I stop just short of touching them. She stares at me with a raw, wanton expression, listening, waiting, wanting.

But I hover, forcing all her senses to focus. She's lost in her passion. Then I blow my breath very softly between her parted lips. I want her to feel it caress the hollowness inside of her.

She inhales deeply, then gasps my name, "Aurelius."

The sensual way she says it draws a moan from my throat, and it sparks a fire in her. Wild eyes challenge me not to resist her as she pushes hard against the hold I have on her chin. Forcing her lips to mine, my hand slides down her jaw, around her ear, and I cup it, allowing her to place her lips on mine.

But I resist giving her the hard kiss she begs me for. My kiss instead is gentle, soft, and firm, all at the same time. She tastes so good. I savor our first connection, drinking in the moment and the sweet sensation of Siri.

When I release her lips, her head falls back into my hand as her body collapses into mine. She stares into my eyes, vulnerable and sincere.

Damn, Wild Thang, I have been looking for you all my life. I slide my fingers between hers, bonding us together.

She whispers, "Thanks ... for the compliment and the kiss."

"Oh, Siri," I hold her tight, squeezing her fingers, breathing on her face, fighting for control of my emotions.

I close my eyes and touch my forehead with hers until I've regained my composure. Then, with a sigh, I release our bond. Gently cupping her face, and cradling it, I place a soft, gentle kiss on her forehead, leaving my lips on her skin as I breathe.

She rests her hands on my waist and squeezes me tight. Understanding that what surges between us is the kind of chemistry that conquers all.

I mumble against her skin. "You're welcome. I meant it."

Then I draw back and look at this woman who owns me. "I better get going."

She sighs and says, "Me too," but doesn't move.

As I reach for the door handle, she says, "Hey.... Moore."

I look back at her. There is a mischievous twinkle in her eyes. A smile breaks across my face as my eyes narrow. "What Wild Thang?"

She giggles with the nickname, then she struts up to me, and I see the Vegas Diva working her assets. She leans her head over, drops her eyes to the ground, and lets them crawl up nice and slow. I smirk, feeling devoured by her diva dominance.

When she looks into my eyes, she informs me, "We have unfinished business, Aurelius. A bottle of Merlot and a raincheck to cash—Sunday!"

I shake my head, laughing, and admit, "I can't wait to open and enjoy that deep, full-body with its enticing flavor. And I've already been dreaming up ways to cash in on the raincheck."

She tosses her hair and sasses, "Mmhmm." Then she struts away.

"Hey, Wright!" I call after her.

She stops and looks back.

"Be safe tonight."

"Of course." She assures me, then she starts walking again.

I add, "Be good too!"

She gives me a sassy wave of her hand and calls over her shoulder. "I'm always good, Aurelius."

I shake my head and whisper, "There is no doubt about that!"

CHAPTER EIGHTEEN

Siri

TD IS PACING as I approach him. When he recognizes me, he smiles and says, "Damn, Siri! You clean up good! But you're late. Get in. We have to go." He walks around to the driver's side and gets in.

I walk to the passenger door. Knowing Aurelius is sitting in the Raptor watching me, I bend over at the waist, keeping my legs straight, and flash him a shadow glimpse of what lies between and beneath before opening the door and getting in.

He whistles an old-fashioned catcall, making me laugh.

As I slide into the Porsche, I look back at him. He's sitting with his tanned, muscular arm resting on the open window, watching me, so I give him a twinkling finger wave.

He grins as I close the door.

Ugh! The car smells of smoke.

"Who is he?" TD asks as he starts the car.

I ignore his question. "I thought we were in a hurry. Let's go."

"We are."

As he backs out, he looks at my dress and grins, "Very sexy!"

"Looking is free, but Rule #1 is still in place." I remind him, then inquire, "Where is this cocktail party anyway?"

He nods and says, "It's behind the Country Club off the golf course. It is super, secluded for privacy, but it's in a restored turn-of-the-century plantation home."

When we pull past Aurelius, he toots the horn a quick tap, then falls in behind us, riding our ass down the drive. His headlights flood the Porsche, and I have to look out the window to keep TD from seeing my smirk.

"Cool!" I rest my hand on my purse, thankful I packed the pistol.

"What the hell does he want?" He looks annoyed in the rearview mirror.

It's pretty obvious to me. Grinning, I chat him up. "I thought of majoring in Architecture briefly, but I ended up getting my degree in accounting."

At the end of the drive, TD signals to make a right turn, and I see in the side mirror that Aurelius also signals that he is turning right. I grin even bigger.

"Really? Why are you a secretary then?" He stops to check the traffic, and the Raptor closes the gap between the vehicles. The interior goes dark as the headlights shine over the top of the car.

"It was a temp job. My mom was in an accident, so I came home while she recuperated."

Annoyed, TD looks in the side mirror. "What the hell is his problem?"

As soon as the traffic clears, he peels out, expecting to leave the Raptor behind, but he can't shake it, so he backs off the gas. "I don't need a speeding ticket, or I would smoke your ass." He glances at me and says, "So you're a boring accountant and not a simple-minded secretary?"

I laugh, "Yep." *Ha! If you only knew who I really am. Your jaw would drop.*

"Thanks again for going with me. I appreciate it," he adds.

"You're welcome. Who else is coming?"

"I doubt you know anyone other than Mandy and Charlie."

"Will Mr. Connors be attending?"

"No, he couldn't make it tonight." He glances at me, and the look in his eye makes my gut tighten. "Listen, Siri. Once we go inside, I'll introduce you to everyone. Then we'll drink and dance. It's an open bar." He grins, hoping that makes me happy.

I stare blankly at him.

"You'll mingle with the men, and then you can leave if you don't want to play. I mean, stay. I just need you to get in. I'll give you my car and hitch a ride with Mandy and Charlie."

Something about his vibe makes the hair on the back of my neck rise. "What the hell kind of cocktail party is this, TD?"

Aurelius

My phone rings. It's Darren. I answer through the Raptor's audio system. "Hey, man. Is there a party tonight?"

"Yeah, you change your mind?"

"No. Sorry, bro. Still not my thing. But I was wondering if a new guy is joining y'all. He goes by the initials T.D."

"Yeah, TD's first time is tonight. Do you know him?" He sounds surprised that I would.

"Not exactly. But he'll be attending alone tonight. I'll explain later." I disconnect the call and hit the gas, instructing my phone app, "Text Siri."

"What do you want to say to Siri?" The phone app asks.

I ride up TD's ass again and flash them with my high beams. I can see they're arguing.

"Pull over."

"Sending Siri a text. 'Pull over.' Ready to send?"

"Yes."

"Sent."

She opens her purse, takes her phone out, and looks back at me. Then she tells him what I sent, holding her phone so he can read it. They argue again, but he hits the brakes and slows down, signaling he's turning into the gas station.

He pulls to the side of the lot, away from the

traffic flow, so I park next to him. Siri and I open our doors simultaneously, but I'm the only one who gets out.

Walking around the front of the truck, I see Siri turned in the seat with a leg hanging out. They are still arguing. So I walk up to TD's door and try the handle.

It's locked. My jaw sets. I lean down and peer in to see what the hell is going on. He's got her by the arm, keeping her from leaving. Her eyes are spitting fire at him. My adrenaline spikes, and I yell as I palm the glass, "Let her go, Motherfucker! She's coming with me."

He jumps, startled by my violent reaction, and looks at me. "Whoa, bro. Wait a minute, now," he says. Then fear freezes his face, and he slowly turns to see Siri pointing a gun at him. His hands fly up.

"No touching means no goddamn touching! You lying, manipulating, little shit!" She spits as she backs out of the car.

As soon as she's clear, the coward peels out, closing her door with the car's momentum, leaving us to stare at each other. She puts the safety back on her pistol and replaces it in her purse as I cross the distance to hold her. Wrapping my arms around her, I hold her tight. She hugs me back.

"He's lucky the damn door was locked!" I say, with my chin on her head.

"No doubt." She leans back and looks up at me. "Thanks for coming to my rescue."

"Are you alright?"

She snuggles up and murmurs against my chest. "Yeah, I'm fine."

I squeeze her tight, "You're welcome."

After a few seconds of cuddling, she pulls away. "I don't want you to be late. I'll call an Uber to take me home. I will wait inside."

I grin down at her, "Or, you can come with me as my date?"

She smirks, then bats her eyes and asks, "You don't mind my tagging along?"

"Hell, no, I don't mind."

She grins, "I would love to be your date."

We walk to the truck, and I open the door for her. The running board slides out, and as she steps onto it, she grabs the overhead handle and pulls her body up. Wiggling in, she gets comfy as I pull the seatbelt out for her. The genuine smile she gives me when she sees I'm holding it ready for her sends my heart into overload. "Thanks," she whispers, then takes the buckle and snaps it in the latch.

I close the door, run around the front of the

truck, climb in, crank it, and put it in gear. Right before I take my foot off the brake, I ask her again. "Are you sure you're alright?"

She looks at her arm and says, "Yeah, he isn't strong enough to leave a mark."

"That's not what I meant." I stare at her and try to imagine what kind of men she's had to deal with as a stripper and what kind of emotional scars there might be because of it.

Siri

He's staring at me with such concern. It's touching, but I don't want him to think I needed his help. I'm not a bimbo. "I'm good, really. Thank you again, though. Your distraction made it easy to get the upper hand."

He looks at me, still concerned, and I add, "I can take care of myself."

"I never doubted that for a moment. But just

because you can handle yourself doesn't mean you are alright. You did draw your weapon on him."

"I'm good, really." Then, add, "It's not the first time I've had to defend myself."

He nods, frowning, so I lighten his burden. I start to laugh. "Aurelius, I wish you could have seen his face when you smacked the window! He may have pissed his pants."

His face relaxes, then he eases out onto the highway, saying, "Well, I wish you could have seen his when you cocked your gun. He probably shit himself when he saw you had it pointed at his crotch."

"I had to aim low. I didn't want to hit you."

"Mmhmm," he laughs. "I'm not sure I believe that."

"Men are more afraid of being shot in their cock than they are of dying. Honestly, just the threat of turning a man from a rooster into a hen usually does the trick."

He laughs out loud. Then he turns on the blinker and enters the Officer's Club parking lot. He pulls into a parking spot and turns the truck off. Then he puts his arm on the center console and turns to face me. He grins and says, "Stay seated. I'm going to open the door for you."

I smile, enjoying the view as he gets out, closes the door, and walks around the front of the truck with the headlights illuminating the Golden God.

Aurelius

I walk around in front of the truck and peer into the cab at her. She lifts her purse strap over her head, then leans down to tuck it under the seat.

When I open her door, she turns to me. I hold my hand up to help her down, but she bypasses it to slide her arms around my neck instead. Then she eases her body down the length of mine, pulling my head down to her lips, and her softness makes everything in me hard for her.

Our lips seal themselves together before her feet hit the ground. Taking my time, I explore her mouth. Her breath gently blows across my cheek as our tongues taste each other.

Then, headlights illuminate us, and a horn blows. *Dammit.*

Jeremy hangs out the window, shouting, "Aurelius! You're my hero!"

Reluctantly, I release Siri's lips and smile down at her twinkling eyes.

She says, "Hero, huh?"

I laugh. "I sunk a three-pointer for the win."

"Ah!" She grins, "I hate I missed it."

"You can watch it on Youtube later." I wink as I slide my hand down her arm and cinch our fingers together. I love how her hand fits mine.

We walk over to greet a tipsy Jeremy and his wife, Diane.

Siri

Jeremy is a hoot, and Diane is so tolerant of him. It's adorable watching them interact. Following them into the Officer's Club, Aurelius continues to hold my hand, and I marvel at how natural it feels. Like we belong together.

Without stopping in the foyer, the four of us

stroll through the dining room and emerge outside onto an extra-large patio. There is a full-service bar against one wall and a banquet table of food against the other. A DJ is jacked up on a platform in the center, and the music he is playing is easy listening music. The patio is crowded with people mingling, eating, and drinking, but not surprisingly, no one is dancing.

We stop inside the door along the outside edge of the dance floor, and Aurelius scans the room. Several men raise their hands to him, and he gives them a head nod, but he doesn't make a move to join them. Instead, he leans down, releasing my hand. I instantly miss it, but he rests it on my lower back, and my tummy tightens with the intimacy.

This man! Even such a small gesture does something to me. I take a deep breath, gathering my desire for him, and putting it firmly into an appropriate place for now. Then look up into his beautiful sapphire blue eyes and wonder how he could still be single.

His deep voice asks in my ear, "Would you like something to drink?"

I have had plenty of interactions with alphas throughout my career, so I understand they like to dominate the small things as well. I ask him, "Are you drinking?"

He nods, "Just one."

"Okay, then. I'll have just one as well."

He grins, pleased that I'm following his lead. And damn, if it isn't a huge turn-on, knowing I can give him pleasure so easily.

"What will it be?" He asks.

"Whatever you're having will be fine." I slowly bat my eyes at him and his hood slightly.

"I like Crown Royal, Regal Apple."

"What?" I laugh, "For real? You're shitting me! I drink that, too."

He chuckles, "Perfect. Two chilled shots are coming up. I'll be right back."

"I'll be right here, waiting." I twinkle up at him, then watch the Golden God's hotness stroll across the dance floor, thoroughly enjoying the view of his powerful thighs and fine ass in his tight white pants. The deep purple shirt accentuates the broadness of his shoulders and his massive, barrel chest. His natural posture is commanding, and although his gait expresses his alpha status, it isn't threatening. It just is.

I know the naked view of this man is going to be life-altering, I laugh.

He is stopped several times along the way by someone shaking his hand or patting him on the back, and the respect his peers show him sends a warm fuzzy feeling through me. Confirming what my gut already knew. He's one of the good guys.

When he steps up to the bar, a man next to him engages him in conversation. He looks back at me, just checking in, and gives me his sexy-as-hell head nod that sends a thrill through me at being acknowledged. He didn't have to, but he did.

I give him my most brilliant smile and lift my head to him too. He grins, and I'm pretty sure he felt the same little thrill. Then he turns his attention to the man speaking to him.

An older, distinguished-looking man, with his wife on his arm, walks up to stand next to me. "Hi, there. I'm Lou."

"And I'm Martha."

"Hi, Lou, Martha. I'm Siri."

"Nice to meet you."

I nod, "You too."

"Are you here with Aurelius Moore?" Martha asks.

"Yes, ma'am."

They exchange a knowing look, then he says, "He's a fine man."

I smile at his confirmation. "I hope so."

Martha says, "We were pleasantly surprised when he walked in with you."

"Oh!" I put my hand to my mouth. "I'm sorry. I didn't realize I would be crashing your event. I apologize."

They exchange another look.

"I was on my way to another party when," I wrinkle my nose, "things went south, and well, Aurelius rescued me." I lift my hands. "So, here I am. I hope that's alright."

They both laugh, and Martha assures me, "Oh, no. That's not what I meant."

Aurelius walks up and greets them, "Colonel, Martha."

Martha's eyes are sparkling when she says, "Aurelius, what a pleasant surprise Siri is."

He hands me my shot, clinks our glasses together, and lifts it with his eyes devouring me. "Yes, she is."

Then, following his lead again, I lift mine, and we drink them at the same time. He in one hit, me in several.

Martha continues, "She was just explaining that you rescued her earlier tonight."

"I did." He laughs as he takes my shot glass back, then sets them both on the table behind us.

Lou reaches out to shake his hand. Aurelius clasps it as Lou says, "Thanks for coming to my rescue tonight as well."

Aurelius tilts his head, and his eyes narrow, then he cuts them to look at Martha, who is grinning from ear to ear. "Why do you say that, sir?"

"Because Martha's had her eye on an expensive purse, and now I don't have to pay for it."

Martha beams at us, then explains to me. "You see, Siri, Aurelius has been stationed here for years, and to our knowledge, meaning the wives in the company, he hasn't dated anyone. Of course, wives talk, and he became our pet project. In the beginning, we tried to set him up, but no one scored." She laughs at him as he shakes his head.

"Then he became the subject of our wild imaginations." She winks at him. "You good-looking son of a bitch. Don't act like you don't know that women of every age drool over you."

He smirks, shakes his head again, and then gives me that killer wink that makes me wet.

"After a few drinks, with a name like Aurelius and a call sign of Hardcore," She wiggles her eyebrows and says, "You can imagine where the gossip went."

And I so can.

"Anyway, somewhere along the line, we began betting on each event whether or not he would be alone when he walked in. Everyone pitched in $20 and had to choose between a date or alone. If he came alone, the pot rolled over. If he remained alone at the end of his tour, we would draw a single winner from that group. But if he came with a date, then those that had bet date would split the money."

I look at Aurelius, and he is stunned. I laugh at him, and he rolls his eyes at me.

Martha says, "Tonight, I went all in for the win. I was the last one, and I gambled big. I chose a date."

She giggles at us, "I won the whole pot."

She hooks Lou's arm. "Now, if you will excuse us, Lou and I have some planning to do."

She says to him as she leads him away, "Not only am I getting that new purse, Colonel, but we're taking vacation compliments of Siri."

CHAPTER NINETEEN

Aurelius

"I CAN'T BELIEVE what I just heard," I chuckle.

Siri giggles up at me as Martha leads Lou away. "Oh, I believe it. Every word. Women talk about men much more than men talk about women."

The music stops, and everyone turns to look at Colonel Capshaw. He addresses the crowd with the DJ's microphone. "Alright, everyone, let's get to the reason we are here."

He pulls his phone out and begins running down

a list of the names of the men and women transferring in, then those that are leaving. When he gets to my name, he says, "And the last man on my list this evening is resigning from the service. Most of you know Aurelius Moore as Hardcore...." And he proceeds to give a rundown on my military service, starting with how I enlisted straight out of high school and went to flight school. He gives the dates and details of my tours in both Iraq and Afghanistan. He includes my citations and medals, then wraps it up by discussing my last assignment as a flight instructor at Fort Rucker.

I glance down several times to see Siri staring at me with that same look on her face she wore when she heard "American Soldier" by Toby Keith playing on my phone. Seeing that look on her face at this moment makes everything I experienced, both good and bad, worth it all.

Colonel Capshaw wraps it up by saying, "Good luck, Aurelius. We thank you for volunteering to serve the greatest country the world has ever known and wish you all the blessings that being a free civilian offers."

The men in the room salute with a "hooah," and there's applause too. I give them a head nod and a quick wave of thanks.

Siri

Wow! I'm shocked at what the Colonel said. Aurelius was involved in an IED explosion that killed another pilot and maimed his crew chief. Instead of seeking cover, he pursued the enemy combatant at significant personal risk to himself. Aurelius surrendered his weapon to the wounded crew chief and then took out the enemy with nothing more than a buck knife.

He's a for-real hero!

The DJ spins "Look at Me" by Carrie Underwood, and Aurelius, the hero, holds his hand out for mine. I take it, and a warm feeling spreads through me. It's different than that first spark of electricity that shot through me when he touched me in the lobby. This one is more powerful than that one.

As we walk onto the dance floor, I realize it's the kind of warm feeling you get when you walk into your home after being away for a long time.

The Golden God pulls me into his arms, hugs me up tight, and we begin to sway slowly. Then he sings the words softly in my ear. The deep tone of his voice is as smooth as butter. Being wrapped up in his essence, feeling his strong arms tenderly holding me, his body heat permeating through my dress, and his intoxicating scent filling my senses, my heart absorbs every word, and my soul soaks them in.

He sings that he's falling for me, and I realize I have already fallen for him. He's something special—someone who only comes along once in a lifetime.

At the end of the song, he cups my face and places a gentle but firm kiss on my lips. The only thing that keeps me from swooning is that I recognize the next song, and I choose the path in that magical moment with him that I want my life to go down.

Kelsea Ballerini sings, "Love Me Like You Mean It," and I hook my arms around his neck and pull his mouth back to mine. Just before our lips touch again, I push him away, step back, and challenge him, singing the words of the song to him.

The grin that spreads across his face tells me I've hit a home run. Sassing him, dancing around him, poking him, rubbing my back up against him, putting on a private dance show just for him, I let him know that if he intends to love me, he has to be worthy. I don't want a one-night stand or a fuck buddy relationship. I want him to mean it.

At the chorus, I roll my right shoulder to the rhythm and slowly lean away, dropping down, drawing him in, inviting him to dominate me.

By the next chorus, he's had enough of my teasing, and he catches me, pulls me hard against his body, and tells me, "Oh, I mean it!"

His hand grasps my ass, and he lifts me, shifting my body weight and forcing me to lean against him. Then we're off dancing.

Wow! He is so smooth. Perfect rhythm and timing. He doesn't exaggerate his movements. He dances the way he walks —with masculine grace. He is in command, and I match his step, crushing my body against his until he spins me away. Then I dance for him until he pulls me back in.

At the end of the song, he dips me, and trusting him, I go limp in his arms, arching my back, letting my head hang. Then I curl my fingers, calling for a kiss.

That sexy sideways grin flashes me, and I know he is mine. Then his kiss proves it, and time stands still.

Aurelius

Kissing Siri is like entering a time warp. No one or nothing else exists. There is only she and I becoming us.

I know the song ended, and everyone is watching, but I don't care. The only one that matters is the one sucking my tongue down her throat.

But then Siri's chest jerks, my tongue is free, and she goes limp in my arms again.

What the hell? I catch her before she falls.

Her chest jerks again ... Ah! To the beat of the next song.

I hold her, staring, fascinated by this talented woman. Then a sexy, soft, breathy moan escapes her lips, "yeah," and my balls draw up. I lift her as her eyes open, and she coos, "woo" with the song.

Then she comes alive and twirls out of my arms to dance her interpretation of the lyrics to Whitney Houston's "I Wanna Dance with Somebody (Who Loves Me)."

My God, she's incredible. She's pushing all my damn buttons. Stomping her feet, jumping to the rhythm, letting go, inviting me to dance with her, but the show is too good to join in.

I'm astonished by her voice too. She sounds a lot like Whitney. Her voice is beautiful, and I wonder if her impersonation skills include singing.

Tossing her head around has her hair slipping out of her knot, and at the very end, she unclips it and shakes her beautiful mane out.

It floats around her like a cloud and transforms her from queen to vixen. She oozes sex in a way that makes women envious, and men fantasize.

Dammit. I have to make this woman mine.

Without missing a beat, the DJ immediately plays "Cake By The Ocean" by DNCE, and my hat goes off to him.

The Wild Thang takes the bait. Pushing her moves to the limits of appropriateness, she withers in front of me, making my cock hard. Needing to feel her against me, I pull her into my arms again to dance. But she shifts gears and dances a salsa for me. I laugh at her ingenious interpretation. She can tease me without offending anyone. And man alive does she ever.

By the time the song ends, I'm thinking of dragging her off the dance floor and taking her in the parking lot. Her eyes twinkle at me, and I laugh. She knows exactly what I'm thinking.

Then the DJ announces, "By special request from Martha to Aurelius, 'One Call Away' by Charlie Puth."

Siri throws her head back and laughs out loud. Then she pokes me in the chest, steps away from me, and begins to dance again. Laughing with her, I step to the beat, grooving while she demonstrates what a dancing diva she is.

The song ends, and the DJ says, "This song goes out to Major Williams and his wife. They are celebrating ten years of marital bliss today." Then, "You Are the Reason" by Calum Scott & Leona Lewis fills the air.

I smile at her, and she smiles back, communicating on a level that doesn't need words.

I open my arms, and she hurries into them. Loving how our bodies meld into one, I grab her ass and tuck her up tight against my cock. A little rougher than I intended, but her fingers dig into my back. She's all in.

Then I step, and she matches me flawlessly.

Dancing with Siri is like dancing with an angel. She is light on her feet, responsive at the slightest direction, limber, and flexible. But above all that, she is beautiful, graceful, and sexy.

We float around the dance floor again, and I marvel at how gorgeous she is. In her glittering gold dress, she looks like a queen. And I am destined to be her king.

The song ends, and I hold her close to me, not letting her go. Knowing, I am never letting her go.

She pushes up on her tiptoes and whispers on my lips. "Let's get out of here."

Siri

Staring into Aurelius's sapphire pools of peace, I have never felt this way before.

Whole.

As the melody begins to play from Whitney Houston's "I Believe In You and Me," he slides his hand down my arm in that sexy way, then bonds me to him. He lifts his head, looks across the dance floor to the dining room, and plots our escape.

As we weave our way between the men and women slow dancing, the song fills my heart, and I stop dead in my tracks.

I don't know why I know, but in that moment, I do.

The world stops spinning.

Aurelius Moore is my one and only. He's my soulmate.

The Greeks believed that we had four arms, four legs, and two faces at the beginning of the human race. But Zeus split us apart, fearing the power of two beings living as one. That's why we spend our lives in search of the one that takes our breath away. Because when we find them, our breath is reunited, and we become one unstoppable soul.

I pause, open my mouth, and softly sing how I feel about him to him.

He turns to look back at me, and the awe on his face says, forever.

Aurelius

MY GOD!

I walk back to her, touch her face gently, and let her fill me with her love. She nuzzles my hand as I stroke her cheek with my thumb.

Staring at her, mesmerized, I realize I've been in love with her from the moment I laid eyes on her. I didn't recognize it until I saw it looking back at me.

Her unique voice is purely her own and not an impersonation. She should be performing on a larger, grander scale. On a stage for fans who love her for who she is, not how amazingly she struts her nearly naked body for them.

She is the real deal, the entire package, and I intend to make all her dreams come true.

When the song ends, she lays her head on my chest, and I breathe with her—not wanting the moment to end.

But the next song pumps everyone around us up. It's "Jungle" by X Ambassadors, and everyone jumps to the beat, holding their hands high.

I run my hand down her arm, clasp our fingers, and escape with her through the dining room and out the front door, not wanting to slow down until I have her alone.

At my truck, I pull her into my arms, slam her

against it, and kiss the hell out of her mouth. My need for her consumes me, and the thought of unzipping my pants right here, and taking her now, enters my brain.

But I know I can't. I can't take her until I come clean. Until she knows when I first fell in love with her and who I am.

So, instead, I end the kiss, open her door, and help her up into the seat.

Siri

Sitting here with my heart bare for the first time in my life, watching Aurelius walk around the front of the truck, my mind drifts back to a conversation I had with my mother when I was young.

"You will find true love one day, I promise."

"But how will I know it's true love?" I asked her, crying because some stupid boy I liked broke my heart.

"You'll know."

"How will I know?"

She smiled and touched my cheek. "Because he will take your breath away."

"But I can't live without breath?"

"Exactly." She said as she put her hands on my face and kissed my forehead. "Now, no more tears. He isn't worth them. He's not the one."

I hugged her tight. "You're the best Mama in the whole world!"

"You'll know him when he comes into your life, Siri, and it will happen when you aren't expecting it."

Aurelius opens the door and gets in.

She was right. I sure wasn't expecting Aurelius Moore.

He cranks the truck, puts it in drive, then eases onto the highway.

"You spoke Italian to me twice tonight, didn't you?" I ask him.

He grins, "I did."

"Do you speak it fluently?"

"I do." He cuts his eyes at me. "My grandparents are Italian."

"What did you say to me in the elevator?"

"Giorno e notte sogno solo di te."

I laugh. "Translation, please."

He laughs too, then tells me. "Day and night, I

dream only of you." He turns to look at me, and his expression says he meant every word.

"Holy Hades! That's... umm hmm."

His grin splits his face. "And ... that is just the reaction I was aiming for."

"Wow!" I admit, "That's so romantic!"

He chuckles, "So, I could have just whispered that in English, and I would have been fine?"

I giggle, "Well, yes, but you scored double points by saying it in both languages."

He checks the traffic and switches lanes.

"Do you have any other siblings?"

"No. Just Ann. You?"

"Only child." I answer, then ask, "Are your parents still alive?"

"Yes. They're in Italy at the moment. Yours?"

"Yes. They're on a sailing trip in the Virgin Islands."

"Sweet. Do you like to sail too?"

"I don't know. I've never done it. I'm a workaholic."

He turns into the private drive of Dogwood Court, and as we ascend, my thoughts about all the bad things I want to do with him flash across my mind.

Aurelius

I pull into the empty parking spot next to her car. "Sit still. I'm going to open your door for you."

"Are you always such a gentleman?"

I look her directly in the eye and give it to her straight-line —not curved. "Negative."

She instantly gets my meaning, and her eyes hood. "Good," she grins.

I open the door and get out, then I trot around to her side. She's sitting with her phone in her hand, and her purse slung over her shoulder, ready.

"Do you like country music?" She asks.

I tilt my head as I help her out of the seat. "Yes."

"Do you know who the Bellamy Brothers are?"

I grin. "I do."

"They have a song called…."

I interrupt her and finish the sentence. "If I said you had a beautiful body, would you hold it against me?"

She grins. "Do you like the song?"

"I do."

She slips her shoes off, hands them to me, and says, "I have a treat for you then."

She cues up the song. Then she steps in place with the soft, fluid motion of a Hawaiian Hula, letting her hips roll, and her arms sensually interpret the lyrics. She pushes her fingers up through her hair for devil's horns and winks at me. Then she forms a circle over her head for a halo, and I shake my head, laughing.

She is such a gifted dancer. So talented. What a waste to be just a stripper.

At the end, she shimmy shakes her tits and ass, turning around and around for me. Then she finishes by adding a circular hair toss that takes my breath away.

Damn! And that's why she's the headlining stripper.

I ask, "Would you?"

She grins, "I will."

When she reaches for her shoes, I hold them up over my head. Then I turn around and squat down. "Hop on. You can ride me to the front door."

She giggles as she jumps on my back, wraps her

legs around my hips, and drapes her arms over my shoulders.

I hook my arms under her legs, needing to feel her skin on my skin. Knowing this is all I'm going to get until I confess, and I'm not ready to risk losing her.

CHAPTER
TWENTY

Siri

OMG! Talk about getting a preview of what's to come.

Dang! Riding him like this, feeling his power moving between my legs, my tits pressing against him, my face inches from his neck! Try not to swoon, Siri! I purr happily. Then I start to giggle.

"What's so funny?"

"This isn't very ladylike. My booty is hanging out of my dress."

He stops immediately, reaching behind to check, but I drop my legs and slide off, then wiggle my dress down to protect my diva-ness from indecent public exposure.

I hold my hand out as he turns around, grinning, "My shoes, please." Then.... "Ohhh!" I squeal as he scoops me off my feet.

Cradling me in his strong arms, I laugh, thrilled, and put my arm around his neck as his strong stride carries me to the door.

His handsome face focused on where we are going gives me the perfect opportunity to study his manly profile. Dark brows frame his sapphire blue eyes with their thick, long lashes. His nose is straight. His lips are sculpted and full but not plump. His jawline is square and firm, not hard. My fingers slide into his thick blonde hair.

Umm! He's Golden God gorgeous.

"Were you named after Marcus Aurelius?"

"No, after my Italian grandfather."

"Your hair looks like a halo."

He chuckles, "Well, trust me when I say I'm no angel."

I laugh, "No, you're a Golden God."

He laughs, "Hardly!"

"That was my first impression of you in the lobby."

He grins, flattered but embarrassed.

"Your sapphire blue eyes are very striking."

"I inherited them from my great-grandmother. Your light, crystal green eyes are as well." His expression is tender, and his voice deep and husky when he says softly, "You are stunning, Siri. Simply stunning."

I tap his massive chest, teasing him. "Flattery will get you everywhere, Aurelius."

His grin is perfection. "How far does honesty take me?"

I roll my eyes and look away. "Umm. It's such a novel concept. Let me think about that."

"Till the end of time?" The depth of his words draws my eyes to his.

"But time is infinite." I hear my husky voice reply.

His head tilts slightly, and a smirk teases his lips. "Exactly."

Sweet Zeus! Try not to swoon, Siri. I rest my hand on his cheek, requesting a kiss, but he denies me. He sets me gently on my feet and gives my stilettos back. He steadies me as I slip them on, then he slides his hand down my arm, eases his fingers between mine, and squeezes. Knowing this is going to be our way of walking together sends a shiver through me. I love being connected to him.

He leads me to the front door, pulls it open, and says, "After you, My Lady."

I grin. That was possessive. I walk through, pulling him with me, not wanting to let go of our connection.

My heels click lightly on the floor, echoing in the late night emptiness, as we walk across the lobby to the elevator.

The sight of the small interior space sends a thrill through me, remembering the ride down earlier. He squeezes my hand, knowing what I'm thinking.

When I enter the elevator, I move to the back but wait while he rests our hands on his ass, pushing the ninth-floor button. I bite my lip, grinning because my hand starts tingling, wanting to squeeze that muscle.

Soon, I promise myself.

As the doors close, I expect him to seduce me, but he doesn't. Instead, he stands silently next to me, staring straight ahead.

Dear God! This is torture! Kiss me already!

I glance at him, but he ignores me. I lean my head back and close my eyes, having a hard time controlling the desire washing over me. Knowing how his body feels pressing into mine, how his kiss tastes, and knowing we are nearing consummation.

I can't imagine what he is waiting for, but then I realize he doesn't want to do it in the elevator, and that is a real possibility if he touches me now.

If he weren't holding my hand, controlling me, I would so take the lead. It's taking every ounce of my willpower to be submissive.

Then I smell his intoxicating scent and hear a low throaty moan that sends a shiver through me. His breath caresses my lips when he whispers, "Did you know?"

"What?" Confused, a scowl forms.

He whispers on my face again. "Did you know?"

I open my eyes to find him staring at me with his other hand bracing the elevator wall, trapping me but keeping his distance.

"About what?" I ask, biting my lip and thinking of stealing a kiss.

"That the cocktail party was a cock and tail sex party of swingers?"

I frown at him, staring into his eyes. Instantly pissed that he would judge me.

He chuckles, "I'm not judging you, Wild Thang. Calm down." He leans in and takes a deep breath of my essence. The hair on my neck stirs and sends a thrill through me, mixing my anger with desire.

Then it hits me. I didn't tell him it was a swinger's party —he knew!

I stiffen, "How did you know that? Are you a swinger?" I blurt out, shocked.

He chuckles, "No, babe. A friend of mine is. I suspected that was where TD was taking you, but I had to wait for confirmation. When I got it, I sent you the text to pull over." He nuzzles my neck, and my knees get weak. Then he nips the skin under my ear, and my eyes roll back in my head. Pulling back to stare into my eyes, he whispers, "I didn't want you going. I don't share."

Being the tease I am, I taunt him. "What if I had wanted to go?"

He grins, "Then I would have convinced you not to."

"And how would you have accomplished that?"

His eyes hood as his hand slides down the elevator wall, wrapping itself in my hair. While he moves our hands up to the small of my back, forcing my tits into his chest. Pinned, he whispers on my lips. "By taming your tail."

My God. His testosterone is oozing from his pores, and I'm wetter than I have ever been before.

The elevator dings before the doors slide open. He lifts me off the wall, and I wrap my legs around his waist. His erection pressing against my clit feels so good, and I crush myself against him.

For a moment, I think he is going to carry me this way down to my apartment, but then he releases my hair and my hand. Sliding his hands over my thighs, careful not to slip inside and touch me, he unhooks my legs.

I drop my heels to the ground. He kisses my hair and leads me out of the elevator to my apartment.

I love how my hand feels in his.

We walk with anticipation without speaking to my door. When we arrive, he releases my hand so I can find my key in my purse and unlock the door. When I swing it open and turn on the light, I reach for him to pull him inside, but he steps back out of my reach.

Floored, I stare at him. "You're not coming in, are you?"

He smiles gently, "No."

"Why not?" I blurt out, disappointment crashing over me. I shake my head, dumbfounded. "I don't understand. Don't you want to?"

A puff of air leaves his chest, and he shakes his head. "I've never wanted to have sex with a woman more. But I need to clear the air first, and if I come in, we'll have sex for sure. I want more with you, Siri, than just a fucking relationship. If we do it now, we won't talk, and then we won't ever talk. I want you to choose to be with me rationally, not just emotionally. I want forever with you if that's possible."

I stand there floored, but not from the temporary rejection. From his openness and honesty. He's being real. He's not playing a game of courtship. He's chosen me as his.

It's overwhelming on the one hand but refreshing on the other. I will never have to guess what this man is thinking and what his intentions are. If I don't know, all I will have to do is ask him. He'll be truthful.

I stare at the man of my dreams, the man who checks all my boxes, but he's just admitted he doesn't share. What if that extends to my career? Will he ask me to stop? I can't imagine a life without dancing. But even if I could, I'm obligated to fulfill my contract.

He backs away, "Goodnight, Siri. Sweet dreams. We'll talk in the morning."

I stand in my doorway, frozen to the spot with so many emotions running through me, watching the

Golden God walk away. When he reaches his door, he puts his key in and opens it. He looks back in my direction and sees me still standing there. He flashes his big, beautiful smile, gives me a simple head nod, and I imagine him saying, "Ciao, Bella." Then he disappears inside.

My shoulders slump as I go into my apartment, shut the door, and turn the bolt. The sound is depressing.

I don't want to be alone again. I don't want to be alone ever again. I want to run down the hall to him. I want Aurelius! But he's right. Once we have sex, that will become the main focus, and issues that should have been brought out into the open and dealt with first won't be.

Secrets as big as the ones I have must be handled before. He has no idea who I am.

Aurelius

Walking straight to the shower, I turn on only the cold water, strip, then step in with my beast leading the way.

The temperature shock reduces the tightness of my erection and the swelling in my balls but does nothing for my need to release the pressure of wanting to take the sexy stripper down the hall in 9A. To claim her. To make her mine.

I hang my head and wonder how in the hell I'm going to tell her the truth and not lose her.

The fact that I walked away just now is proof of how much she means to me. Being with her tonight, seeing her smile, hearing her giggle, watching how sweet she is, and learning how good a person she is only made me want her more. If I can make her mine, we will be unstoppable together.

I grab the bar of soap and lather up. Washing away my sins, cleansing myself of my past, knowing there will never be another now. Siri is my everything.

My hand slides down my shaft as the vision of her flashes like a movie behind my eyelids, and I stroke my cock until he explodes. Then I stand there, breathing, better able to reason, but knowing I'm not going to sleep tonight.

I dry off, wrap the towel around my waist, go into the kitchen, and realize I left the cooler of beer in the back of the truck.

With nothing to drown my sorrows with but the bottle of Merlot I'm saving to share with Siri, I take the milk out and pour myself a tall glass. But as the thick white liquid splashes in, I see the sexy minx dipping her cookie in it, and my cock gets hard again.

I hang my head. I'm fighting a losing battle.

Siri

I step out of the shower, unwrap my hair from the towel, then dry off with it. Too keyed up to rest, I decide to make myself a cup of Tension Tamer tea.

In the kitchen, I turn a stove burner on. Fill my tea kettle with water, set it on top of the eye to boil, then open the cabinet, remove the box of tea bags, and pick one. Then take my Surreal coffee mug from the drainer, and place the tea bag in it.

DING! DING!

I freeze.

Could that be Aurelius?

I spin around. My phone is still in my purse.

Of course, it's him! Who else would it be this time of night?

Running into the bedroom, I dive onto my bed, snatch my phone from my purse, and laugh aloud. Giddy as a schoolgirl, I smile at my phone.

are you still up?

I giggle as I roll onto my back and hold it in the air to type.

Yes, I'm fixing myself a cup of Tension Tamer tea.

I hit send, roll off the bed, and walk back into the kitchen with my phone in my hand. Before I arrive, it dings again.

I can't sleep either. I like tea, but I like taming tail better.

I stare at the phone. Oh, Holy Hades! Here we go!

I smile and type feverishly, teasing him.

So you think you're the man for the job?

YES.

The teapot starts to whistle, and I jump. As I pull the water off the stove, my phone dings again.

Your teapot is whistling.

Sweet Zeus! Father of the Gods! He's outside my door!

My heart falls to my feet.

My breathing stops completely.

I rush to the door and peek out the peephole. What I see stops time.

The most gorgeous man on the planet is leaning against the wall, looking at his cell phone with only a white towel wrapped around his waist. His hair is tousled and still wet, but the lightest strands, drying first, shine brightest, reflecting the harsh hallway lights like a halo.

His entire body is without tan lines. It is the same golden color as his hand, and he is ripped! Not just muscular and defined, but ripped!

From his bulging arms to his pumped perfect pecs, to his teres majors that form his sharp body triangle, to his tight, clearly defined, eight-pack abs to his molded exposed v-shape that points to his package. He is shredded.

My mouth waters.

A body that perfect should never wear clothes!

He looks so damn hot I nearly faint! I turn my back and lean against the door, take a deep breath, and type.

Just a minute. I'm naked. Let me grab my robe.

My mind races with all the thoughts of what I need to say to him first, but my heart pounds wildly in my chest, and my body tells my mind to shut the hell up. The time is at hand. It's happening now!

I look back through the peephole at his nearly naked body. He is unbelievably BEAUTIFUL!

He reads my text and then starts to type.

I look down with the ding.

No. No robe. That's the way I want you.

He smiles up at the door, and a thrill that feels like jumping out of a perfectly good airplane hits me. Like a million butterflies fluttering free inside, and I nearly drop my phone.

I spin back around to brace against the door, trying to compose myself. Despite my nerves, I smile. I take another deep breath and look out the peephole again. He is staring at the door, waiting for me to open it with such intensity that it reaches the depth of my soul.

And I realize, if I don't, Aurelius is going to bust it down. He's not going to be denied. I am his. I lay my hand on the lock and turn it as I peek again at him.

When he hears it moving, he pushes off the wall, and the flexing and rippling muscles make me bite my lip hard.

WOW! He is majestic!

With one smooth motion, he strides across the distance, commanding and yet relaxed.

He turns the knob, unlatches the door, then pushes it open, stepping inside without hesitation. His commanding presence fills the foyer, and he drops his phone on top of the white towel.

My knees nearly buckle again at the sight of his naked perfection. His smile sends those million butterflies flying around inside me again, but this time they are flying fast and furious in my treasure box.

"Hi," I whisper.

His eyes take their time, traveling slowly up the same path as in the elevator earlier. Taking in every detail of my nakedness.

Being bare and being devoured like this sends a surge of wildness through me, and when he looks me in the eye, I challenge him.

CHAPTER TWENTY-ONE

Aurelius

THERE IS IT. That 'take me now' expression.

Oh, Wild Thang, I do intend to!

As I advance, her phone slips from her fingers and lands softly on the carpet at her feet. Inches away, I stop, towering over her. She slides her hands up my chest and around my neck. Then cups my face and pulls my lips to hers. She opens her mouth wide, inviting my tongue inside. I thrust it, filling her mouth, and she sucks it hard, demanding more. Pulling a primal groan from my throat.

I wrap my hand in her hair and pin her with my body against the wall. She releases my tongue, and I smile down on her.

I bury my face in her neck and inhale her essence. Then whispering against her skin, I confess. "I shouldn't be here, but I can't stay away any longer."

I nibble her neck, and she moans as little goosebumps rise to greet my lips.

"I want you, Aurelius," she whispers.

"Mmm," I suck her neck and mark her as mine.

Her breathing changes into little short snatches of uncontrolled excited breath.

I lean back to look into her eyes. When hers lock onto mine, they focus, and the lost wild thang finds peace.

A depth of emotion I have never experienced before stirs inside me, and my lips possess hers, needing to be one with her. As we kiss, I feel her relax, her breath syncs with mine, and when I look into her eyes again, I see a calm need.

"Good girl," I whisper, and she smiles.

I begin again, placing little nibbles along her jawline, traveling back to her neck. Licking, then sucking her skin gently into my mouth, then nibbling her flesh, I seduce her. Moving lower and lower until I'm devouring her ripe nipples. She loses her breath again, moaning and panting, begging without words.

I capture her mouth. "We have time. There is no need to rush this. Let's take it nice and slow. Breathe, baby."

I release her hair, run my hand down her arm, and cinch our fingers together, then I back away and pull her off the wall. "I want to make this unforgettable with you. I want to erase all memories from your mind. I want to replace everything, and everyone, like you have for me. I want to be your one and only lover."

Her eyes are locked on mine. She wants to belong to me.

I pull her into my arms, then lift her off her feet, cradling her. Her hand caresses my face. Then her fingertips trace my lips as I carry her to the bed.

I lay her gently down and stare at the most exquisite creature I have ever seen. Her long blonde hair fans out over the pillows, and her bronze-toned body stands out against the white sheets. Her beautiful nipples are the same color as her lips, and I know that I will find the same dark pinkness when I push her legs open.

She stares up at me with her crystal green eyes and dark arched brows.

"It's not possible," I tell her.

Her brows furrow and her eyes search mine.

I crawl onto the bed and stretch my body next to hers. Then I tell her, "You are more beautiful than my dreams of you."

I lower my mouth to suckle her tips, and her moans of pleasure fill all the emptiness inside me.

As I tease them, flicking and licking, then sucking and nibbling, she begins to quiver with the overload of sweet sensation after sweet sensation. When her back arches and she pushes them up for more, I slide my hand down to her clit.

Hovering my hand above it, my lips tease her taut tip when I say, "And I have dreamed of you every hour of every day since I first laid eyes on you."

I bite, and she bucks. Her clit crashes into my hand, and her moan is what gives men power. Working my kisses and nips down, my hands push her legs open. She lifts her head off her pillow to watch me go down on her, and when I do, her head falls back, and she thanks God for making her a woman.

As I work, her hands grip the sheets, and she

moves against my face, showing me the rhythm that is pleasing to her.

But then, she bucks her hips, throwing me off balance, hand shucks my waist, and before I realize what's happened, the pole dancer flips me over, and her lips suck my cock into her mouth.

Siri

His sharp intake of air, and then his paralysis as he holds it in, is followed by a deep, majestic moan as I slowly slide his entire cock down my throat. Evidence of how women enslave men.

His groan of "S...I...R...I" is the sexiest sound I have ever heard! I work him over until he's ready to blow, and he flips me like a feather. Then spins and pins me under him.

"Wild Thang," his eyes bore into mine, holding my gaze.

"Aurelius, I have dreamed of you every day of my life."

If a man's heart melts as a woman does, then his just did. He closes his eyes and whispers, "Sweet Thang." Then his lips are on mine again, and he owns all of me.

Understanding what drives me wild now, he gives it to me. Playing with my breasts, flicking, licking, sucking, nibbling, making my body squirm with desire for him. He sets me on fire, and my blood is pounding in my ears.

"Birth control?" He asks.

"Since 16."

Then he starts downward, and the anticipation heightens the sensual sensation of his kisses. When he arrives, he teases me until I purr his name. “A..u..r..e..l..i..u..s.”

Aurelius

Siri begs me, "Aurelius, please! Take me. Take me now."

Knowing this is claiming, I kneel in her zone and warn her with a promise. "Hang on, baby. I'm going to take you to heaven."

"Yes! Yes, Aurelius."

Because I'm big and don't want to rip her, I lean forward, lining up, intending to slide in nice and slow.

She encourages me, "Come on, baby. Do it!"

I push, but.... What the hell?

She squirms under me. "Make me yours, please!"

I glare at her as comprehension dawns on me. No way! No damn way! You've got to be kidding me. I run my fingers over her slit to confirm it. "Damn! You're a virgin?"

I rear back on my heels, shaking my head, gobsmacked. "My mind is blown."

She reaches for me, "Aurelius, come take me to heaven. I want you to be my first time."

I flop onto my back, put my arm over my face, and tell the room. "Dammit! I fucked up."

She crawls over to me and says, "I'm sorry you're so shocked. I was hoping it would just happen."

I look at this beautiful woman with her gorgeous mane of platinum blonde hair and perfect tits hanging down. Damn, she's even more special than I thought. "I don't know what to say, Siri. I'm gobsmacked. Give me a minute to absorb this, okay?"

She rolls on top of me, flattening her body against mine, and kisses my chest. My heart stirs with her affection.

She makes her case to continue, "You said it all when you said you wanted to make this unforgettable with you."

She grins a cute sideways grin, "Well, it will be."

She nips my skin, and I finch. "You said I want to be your one and only lover. You will be."

She drags her body up and rests her nose on mine, then pecks my lips. "I'm not completely sealed. I use tampons. But I've never been penetrated by anyone."

"Hmm." The air lodged in my chest escapes. "This changes everything, though.

She blinks, and her brows furrow, confused. "You still want me, don't you?"

I reach around her, pinning her to me. "Of course, I want you. I've wanted you since the first time I saw you." I lift my head and peck her perfect pouty lips. "But...."

"But what?" She frowns.

"You're innocent, and I am anything but innocent."

"Are you serious?" Her angry eyes stare at me and she pushes me away.

Shocked, I release her, and she sits up, glaring at me, then rolls off.

"Wild Thang, why are you so angry?" I rise on my elbow and reach for her, but she doesn't take my hand.

"I'm not innocent, Aurelius. You're acting like you're going to STEAL it from me because I'm too stupid to know what I want and who I want to finally fuck!"

Her words stun me.

She points her finger at my chest for emphasis, "You should be honored, Aurelius!"

Her words slap me.

"I'm giving you something I've treasured and protected my entire life!"

She glares down at me. "I'm still a virgin because I'm a disciplined person. I love myself. I respect myself. But I'm not innocent, Aurelius. I know more about sex than most people who have had sex for fifty years."

I listen to her rant, but I'm stoic.

"Gawd!" She grits her teeth. "My virginity is my call, and I'm calling your name."

"Listen, Siri. This is *our* call. I am honored, but you need to know everything about me."

She sasses, "I know the most important thing. I know I want it to be you!"

"You know what I mean," I tell her.

"Look," she says, calming down a little bit. "I appreciate the fact that you are wanting to get this right because you understand what I'm giving you. So, get on with it. Tell me what I need to know right now. No more stalling. Give me the brutal hardcore truth. Because you're not leaving here without taking my virginity."

I laugh, "That's a pretty straight-line —no curves delivery."

She frowns, "What?"

I explain, "Typically, that's how I communicate. Concise brutal honesty. Straight-line —no curves delivery."

"Great! Give it to me straight-line —no curves then."

"Siri," I pause, "I'm afraid you'll get mad and leave without hearing me out." I hold my hand out for hers. "I'm not telling you until I'm holding you in my arms."

She crawls back over, pushes me down, and straddles me. I flip her before she can react and pin her down.

"What I'm going to tell you is going to make you mad. Not because it's bad or anything, but because I kept it from you, and the only reason I did was that the truth would have prevented your learning who I am. You implied people judge you based on your profession as a Vegas dancer. Well, people judge me because of *who* I am."

"Who are you that they would misjudge?"

I sigh, "I'm the heir to the Italian Liotine fortune."

"What?"

"One day, I'll be the head of the Italian family business."

"You're mafia?" She asks, shocked.

I tilt my head. "We are not criminals. More like a dynasty." I cautiously lean over for a kiss, and she puckers up for me, giving me a butterfly peck.

Her eyes narrow. "So, you're rich?"

"Yes."

"You don't have a stuck-up bone in your body. Well ... you do have one." Her eyebrow cocks, making me laugh. "How rich? Filthy rich? 'Cause I like filthy."

I grin down at her. "Yes. We're filthy rich."

"I'm not intimidated by rich people, Aurelius. They, you, put your pants on the same way as everyone else. As long as you aren't criminals."

"We're not, but the business is worth billions."

"Billions with a B?"

"Yes."

She shakes her head. "How in the hell do you manage to fly under the radar?"

"Well, I enlisted in the Army before I graduated from high school, and there's this unspoken rule in the press corp that affords the rich, when they serve in the military, to keep our privacy protected."

"What made you enlist so young?"

"My next confession."

She smiles, "Okay, so, you're a billionaire heir. What else?"

"At eighteen, I was considered Italy's most eligible bachelor. That's why I rushed to enlist. I wanted to define myself. Not be defined by my family's wealth."

"And... now you're resigning, and you'll be fair game."

"Yes."

"Well, I know all about the pressures of being a celebrity and dealing with the press. Not a deal breaker either."

"There's one thing left." I squeeze her tight. "Don't get mad. Hear me out."

She nods, but her eyes are suspicious.

"I'm a Venture Capitalist. I'm rich in my own right. My business partner asked me last fall to check you out before he invested in an opportunity Bart was offering."

"So.... You've known all along I'm a stripper?"

I nod. "I feared that if you knew that I knew who you were, you would assume I was a stalker."

"Hmm. Knowing would have changed everything."

"Exactly. That's why I haven't told you any of this before. Fate had seen fit to put you on my turf, and I would take you on my terms. You've met the man I truly am. I haven't lied to you about anything."

"Did you invest?"

"No, I didn't invest. But my friend did."

She frowns, "Why not?"

"I didn't want any conflict of interest." I peck her lips. "The night I saw you dance changed my life. Since then, I have thought of you, and only you, every hour of every day. I left that first show knowing I had to have you. I booked a VIP room and had to wait three months. Then, you vanished, and I was crushed. Beverly encouraged me to cancel, but I wouldn't. I have never reacted to a woman as I have to you, and I wasn't willing to let you go. I'm obsessed." I grin.

She chuckles, "Hardcore commitment."

"Affirmative. Imagine my shock when you walked across the parking lot in front of me. I couldn't believe it. There you were. You dropped your keys, and they went under your car. You bent over to get them, and, man," I grin at her. "You were panty-less."

"Oh, wow!" She says. "I flashed my diva-ness?"

"You did, and it was perfect!" I chuckle. "I went to Dogwood Court to rent an apartment for my buddy and left knowing I was moving out of my house on the farm and in there myself. I set about seducing you, wooing you, to win your heart. I was going to do everything in my power not to screw up the opportunity to make you mine —forever."

"You were right to confess first. So I have to come clean too. I'm not simply Seary, the stripper, the headlining act at Been Jammin's. I'm Surreal. The Star of the Vegas Strip." She pauses, letting that sink in.

"How in the hell do you pull that off? It would be physically impossible."

She laughs, "Wigs, makeup, props, ropes, pulleys, lifts. I have a fabulous team."

"Wow, Wild Thang, you are so much more than I dreamed of."

She whispers, "Kiss me."

I give her what she asks for.

Aurelius

My hands slip behind her back so I can lift her tits to my mouth. I latch on and tease one, then the other, making her moan for me.

"Oh my god, that feels so good." Her fingers caress my scalp while I suckle her tits.

But then she says, "Aurelius, you can't tame my tail," and I realize she is still thinking about us and not lost in my seduction. I lift my face to look into her eyes. They are hooded but focused.

Her breathy voice says, "I can't give up dancing. Please don't ask me to."

I crawl up her body to stare into her eyes. "Don't

worry. I won't." I peck her lips, hoping to kiss away her thoughts, but she doesn't open her mouth. Instead, she flips me over onto my back. Then she goes down on me, pushing my cock down her throat.

The moan that escapes my mouth is loud and long.

As she moves between my legs and settles in to work me over, she says, "But you said you don't share."

Then she goes down on me again. My head falls back with the pleasure she's giving me, and I have to fight to focus my thoughts. When she releases me, I lift my head and look at her. "I don't."

Her big eyes hold mine as she licks me. "But how are we going to make this work?"

I sit up, snatch a handful of her hair, and pull her off my cock. She smirks as I force her lips to mine.

"You don't understand." I grip her throat and gently squeeze as I thrust my tongue in her mouth. She latches on, sucking it deep, telling me how she wants me to take her.

I flip her over, and she wraps her legs around me, riding me down.

I end the kiss, staring into her eyes, and tell her, "I don't mind if you dance naked as a jaybird.

Because I'm going to not only tame your tail but claim it as mine."

Then I let her go, and she spreads her legs wide for me as I spit on my cock and line up. Then I thrust firmly past her virginity and assure her, "Tu sei mio perché io sono tuo. [You are mine because I am yours]."

Siri

The resistance is minimal. The pain nothing compared to the sensation of pleasure that sweeps over me, shutting out everything else. I gasp with the feeling of fullness. Then a loud moan escapes my lips when he hits bottom.

He feels so good inside me!

He stops, unsure, hesitating, listening to my moan. Then he slowly withdraws.

I gasp small breaths of blissful air, then grab his ass with both hands and pull him into me. "Don't stop! Go, baby, go!"

His thrust hits bottom again, and my eyes roll back in my head.

His body covers mine entirely, and I bury my face in his neck, smelling his scent, filling every part of my being with him.

He gives me what I want, and my body responds, matching his rhythm, as we climb the mountain of passion.

'My God' starts as a mantra but soon becomes 'My Golden God' as he tames my tail and claims me.

At the peak, I stop moving my hips, arch my back, throwing my arms to the bed, grabbing the covers, and straining for release.

He pushes his body off mine. Bracing his torso on his arms, he withdraws his full length, then drives himself deep, pounding me over and over again with jarring force until I scream with exquisite release. "A... U... R... E... L... I... U... S...!"

As the first wave of a mind-shattering orgasm washes over me, my screaming his name sends him shooting for the stars, and I scream out again. "YES! YES! YES! OH MY GOLDEN GOD!"

He hammers me until we are both fully satisfied. Then he falls on me, spent and exhausted, having given me all of himself.

I stroke his hair, caressing his temple with my

thumb while he recovers. His face buried in my neck, his breathing deep and powerful.

When he stirs, he rolls onto his back, puts an arm under his head, and pulls me to cuddle with him. I move on my side and trace my finger down his golden torso, laying my face on his chest.

He chuckles, "Golden God."

I giggle, "Affirmative."

"I'm not sure how I feel about that title."

He chuckles again as I curl up, smiling, draping an arm over his chest, hugging him, and closing my eyes to sleep. "If I'm your Wild Thang, you're my Golden God."

He whispers as he kisses the top of my head. "Ok, I am your Golden God because you are most definitely my Wild Thang."

Sometime later, I rouse from deep sleep to feel Aurelius pull me to spoon with him, and I hear him whisper in my ear. "Forevermore, my Every Thang."

Thank you for reading

DECEIT

I hope you enjoyed Aurelius and Siri's love story thus far and will choose to leave a review for others.

TRUTH

THE CONCLUSION OF AURELIUS AND SIRI'S LOVE STORY

Chapter One

Siri

A pilot emerges from the jet with a big smile and walks over to greet us. "Moore! Man, it's good to see you! How've you been?"

"Good, Morris. And you?"

"No complaints. Who's this beautiful lady you have on your arm?"

"This is *my* lady." He says it possessively. "Siri Wright. Siri, allow me to introduce you to the first scoundrel I met in flight school, Mike Morris."

He nods, "Nice to meet you. Although, I'm surprised. Moore here has been a lone wolf as long as I've known him."

"He was just waiting for the Wright one." I wink at Morris, then I glance over my shoulder at Aurelius and he gives me that killer wink. I smirk, roll the peppermint I popped in my mouth after his blowjob on the way to the airport around my tongue so he can see it, then turn to walk up the stairs.

Morris says to him, "Must have been. You look different. Relaxed. It looks good on you."

When we enter the cabin, I'm pleasantly surprised at the luxury. The seats are dark leather and plush. Mary, the flight attendant, says, "Sit anywhere. You are our only passengers on this trip."

Aurelius sits and offers me the window seat. I snuggle in under his arm and smile at Morris. He laughs and shakes his head, amused. "It's good to see him happy, Siri. Well, let me get us airborne and heading to Rome."

We buckle up, and as soon as the plane moves, my nose is glued to the window. Aurelius holds my hand and watches me. I look at him and grin, "I love watching the world change."

He grins back. "You enjoy every moment of every day, don't you?"

"I try to. Why wouldn't you? Your heart only has so many beats. You better enjoy them."

He brings my hand to his lips and kisses it. I turn back to stare out the window.

Once we've reached cruising altitude, Mary appears with blankets and pillows. We kick off our shoes, and Aurelius takes his tie off.

I ask as soon as we settle in. "So this party of what would have been your Grandfather's 85th birthday?"

"Not just a party. It's a celebration."

"Oh. What's the difference?"

"Big and extravagant. We go all out for it each year, making it a family reunion and keeping the tradition he established alive. He would say that it's the Texan in him coming out." Aurelius laughs.

"Texan? I thought he was Italian?"

"He claimed both. It's a great story. Especially the part about courting my grandmother. 'It's quite the love story.'" Aurelius says with a slow southern drawl with just a hint of an Italian accent.

"Tell me the short version, please. It will make a good bedtime story."

"My grandmother was a gifted dancer —like you. She was a ballerina. They met and fell in love, but she wouldn't give up her career for him. At first, his heart was broken, he took a job with this big company, and they transferred him to Texas. He saved his money, bought some land, then struck oil. When he returned to Italy years later as a wealthy oil baron, he reconnected with my grandmother and asked her again to marry him. Again, she refused because of her career. But this time, she told him she would marry him when she was too old to perform. Each year he returned and asked her. Finally, she agreed. They wed, and she moved to Texas with him. They had my mother a year later and lived happily ever after until she died. He returned to Italy to bury her and stayed. He wouldn't leave her again." Aurelius speaks with the same funny accent. "Till death do us part. Well, I'm not dead." Aurelius laughs, "He was quite the character."

"Wow. That is a romantic story. Tell me about your parents."

"My mother is Zita. My dad is Robert. Everyone calls him Bob. They met in high school, fell in love, and got married. Bob joined the Army. They had me, then Ann. We were Army brats until middle school. He resigned from the military to help his parents run the farm." He yawns. His grin is lazy, and his eyelids are heavy. "Siri, I'm drained. I'll share more later."

I slide in next to him, aware that Mary is watching us, and she dims the cabin lights. Before I can get the blanket pulled up, he softly snores beside me. I put his arm over me and snuggle against him. His gentle snoring lulls me to sleep.

The next thing I know, Mary is waking us with a fresh cup of coffee, and the sun is shining in the cabin windows. Aurelius stretches and stands. He takes the coffee she offers. "How long till we land?"

"About an hour. Our shower gives 40 minutes of hot water." She tells us as she hands me coffee. "There are toiletries in the bathroom. I've placed your carry-on luggage inside. Let me know if you need anything else. There are also breakfast muffins and fruit if you want to eat."

"Thank you," he tells her. "Please bring my phone. We'll enjoy our coffee, then shower. No breakfast."

She retrieves it for him, and I watch him check his emails. When he places a call, he speaks Italian, and I drape his arm around my shoulders like a shawl and flex his fingers as I examine them, listening to his crisp business voice.

When he hangs up the phone, he tells me. "I'm happy you are with me."

My heart melts. "I will follow you anywhere, Aurelius."

He chuckles, "But you have to return to Vegas by May first."

"Yes, it'll be your turn to follow me."

He places a butterfly kiss on my forehead. "I've reserved a table at Gia's for breakfast. We'll grab a bite, then sightsee."

I squeal softly, clapping my hands together fast. "I can't wait!"

He chuckles as he stands and stretches. "Fun Thang, let's go get cleaned up."

He pulls me under the water. When I'm wet and relaxed, he turns the shower off and picks up the bottle of body wash. He squirts a huge handful, then sets it back down, lathers my back, and then down to my ass, cupping and massaging my butt cheeks.

His hands are gentle and firm, like his lips when

they kiss me. Then he turns me around, leans my back against him, and starts at my throat. He bathes each arm down to my fingers, cinching his with mine.

I love how it makes me feel connected.

Then working his way back up, I moan as he runs his hands down the sides of my waist to the front of my tummy.

I thread my fingers over his and roll my hips with his rhythm. Our bodies slide against each other, slippery and sexy. I arch my back and lay my head on him, pushing my big ass around his erection. It slides easily between my cheeks, and I squeeze them together, capturing it. Then I flex and release with a slight roll of my hips and massage him.

"Oh, damn!" I hear in my ear.

He squeezes his fingers together, ensuring mine stay entwined, then he slides them up to my breasts, where we massage them, matching my rhythm. The feeling of sharing our seduction this way is indescribable.

He and I are one.

"Hold on, Wild Thang. I'm not finished bathing you." He squats down and runs his hands up and down both legs.

I feel like purring, but I sigh. Competence is a beautiful thing!

He pulls me to his chest, turns the water on, and moves us under it. The cold water runs down his back and splashes off his shoulders, so I close my eyes. The world disappears, and immediately, my breathing matches his. I feel his fingers pushing my hair out of my face again, then he cups my chin and lifts it to receive his kiss.

There is only Aurelius.

"The water is warm now. Relax." He steps to the side, and the warm water caresses me.

He holds my hair while the water runs through it. Then he washes the soap away. Gently lifting my arms, then my legs, his caring touch makes me drop all defenses and lean on him. All the while, he repeats these phrases. "You are stunning, Siri.... Beautiful Baby.... Perfect.... Mine...."

My heart melts with the sincerity of his words as they fall deep inside, touching me where no one else has ever been before.

He squats, hooks my legs, lifts me, then slams me into the shower wall, ramming his cock deep. The penetrating stab sends a pleasurable shock through me, satisfying my wild nature like nothing before.

I hook his neck with my arms and moan.

"Shhh! Wild Thang," he says softly, "I got you."

The closer to bursting he gets, the harder he becomes and the better the stroke inside me. He goes full throttle, moving fast and furious, making my teeth rattle and sending me spiraling out of this world. The feeling is unbelievable!

He slowly lets my legs down and pulls me against him, holding me up as he releases my body from the wall. We breathe together.

Staring at him with his eyes closed, enjoying the afterglow, I marvel at him. He is so sweet and kind.

"Good girl," he utters, then kisses my head. He pulls me under the water, and we wash our juices away.

Thirty-five minutes later, we're back in our seats. My nose is to the window, and Aurelius is on his laptop. The 'fasten your seatbelt' symbol illuminates. Mary appears from behind the curtain to ensure we are aware. Then she disappears again. Morris keys the intercom and begins narrating the sights we are flying over as we approach Rome.

"I'm so excited! I've dreamed of this day for a long time!"

"I'm glad I'm making your dreams come true."

My eyes leave the sights. I lean over and place my lips on his. His hand slides around my ear. "You are," I whisper.

Morris is at the door when we exit. He and Aurelius agree to get together when they are both stateside again. We pass without a hitch through customs, and finally, I get my passport stamped in Italy.

A limo awaits us. Aurelius introduces me to his driver, Angelo. Then, as we are whisked away to the hotel, he gives me the itinerary. "My apartment is under renovation, so we will stay at the Hotel Aldo. We'll eat a nice breakfast, then do some shopping. We'll fill the remainder of the weekend sightseeing before heading to the family villa."

As the limo pulls out, I stare out the window. "How long have you lived in Rome?"

"Off and on my whole life."

"I'm living a dream!" I hold my arm out to him. "Pinch me."

He pretends to pinch it, then kisses it. "You may be living a dream, but you're not dreaming. I promise. You are in Rome."

When we pull up to the curb, the doorman opens my car door. I take his hand to exit, walk away a few steps, and wait for Aurelius to tip him, then join me. Walking in, the beauty and splendor of the Hotel are everything and more than I would expect. It is posh with an Old World grandeur that Vegas can't replicate.

Continue reading
Truth

Cindee Bartholomew

BILLIONAIRE Books ROMCOM

FEATURED ON:

Cindee Bartholomew gives her readers the perfect blend of steam, sass, and soul.

She also writes as Jessika Klide and Stingray23.

Made in the USA
Columbia, SC
11 June 2025

59273855R00198